Emir promised pleasure. He promised forgetfulness. And for however short a time the prospect of that seemed preferable right now to doing battle endlessly on ever

How would it feel  her and have thos pleasure?

She must have swayed towards him, for the next thing she knew he was holding her in front of him.

'Why, Britt,' he said. 'If I'd known we could have arranged something before the meeting.'

He was blunter than she had ever been—blunter than she was prepared for—and breath shot out of her lungs as he dipped his head to brush her lips with his. Incredibly, she was instantly hungry, instantly frantic for more pressure, more intimacy, and for everything to happen fast.

He felt so good…so very good.

She wanted this. She needed it. And she forgot everything the moment his hands caressed her breasts. She wanted this—wanted him. She wanted, just for once in her life, to feel that she didn't have to be the leader, the fighter, that just this one time she could be a woman.

Susan Stephens was a professional singer before meeting her husband on the tiny Mediterranean island of Malta. In true Modern™ Romance style they met on Monday, became engaged on Friday, and were married three months after that. Almost thirty years and three children later, they are still in love. (Susan does not advise her children to return home one day with a similar story, as she may not take the news with the same fortitude as her own mother!)

Susan had written several non-fiction books when fate took a hand. At a charity costume ball there was an after-dinner auction. One of the lots, 'Spend a Day with an Author', had been donated by Mills & Boon® author Penny Jordan. Susan's husband bought this lot, and Penny was to become not just a great friend but a wonderful mentor, who encouraged Susan to write romance.

Susan loves her family, her pets, her friends and her writing. She enjoys entertaining, travel, and going to the theatre. She reads, cooks, and plays the piano to relax, and can occasionally be found throwing herself off mountains on a pair of skis or galloping through the countryside.

Visit Susan's website at www.susanstephens.net— she loves to hear from her readers all around the world!

If you love reading about the Skavanga family dynasty, take a look at their website:
http://www.susanstephens.com/skavanga/index.html

Recent titles by the same author:

TAMING THE LAST ACOSTA
THE MAN FROM HER WAYWARD PAST*
A TASTE OF THE UNTAMED*
THE ARGENTINIAN'S SOLACE*

*Titles linked to the Acosta Family

**Did you know these are also available as eBooks?
Visit www.millsandboon.co.uk**

DIAMOND
IN THE DESERT

BY
SUSAN STEPHENS

First published in Great Britain 2013
by Mills & Boon, an imprint of Harlequin (UK) Limited.
Harlequin (UK) Limited, Eton House, 18-24 Paradise Road,
Richmond, Surrey TW9 1SR

© Susan Stephens 2013

ISBN: 978 0 263 90016 3

DIAMOND
IN THE DESERT

For all my wonderful readers
who love the mystery of the desert
and the romance of a sheikh.

CHAPTER ONE

MONDAY SEVEN A.M. on a cold, foggy day in London a breakfast meeting was being held by a powerful consortium set up to acquire the world's biggest diamond mine. The group of three men was led by Sheikh Sharif al Kareshi, a leading geologist otherwise known as the Black Sheikh, thanks to his discovery of vast oil lakes beneath the desert sands of Kareshi. Concealed lighting was set at the perfect level for reading the fine print on a contract, and the surroundings were sumptuous as befitted the ruling Sheikh of Kareshi in his London home. Seated with the sheikh at the table were two men of roughly the same age, that was to say, thirty-two. One was a Spaniard, and the other owned an island off southern Italy. All three men were giants in the world of commerce, and heartbreakers in the game of life. Colossal sums of money were being bandied about. The atmosphere was tense.

'A diamond mine beyond the Arctic circle?' the darkly glamorous Count Roman Quisvada remarked.

'Diamonds were discovered in the Canadian Arctic some years back,' Sharif explained, leaning back. 'Why not the European Arctic, my friend?'

All three men had been friends since boarding school in England, and, although they had all gone on to make individual fortunes, they were bound by friendship and trusted each other implicitly.

'My first pass over the findings suggests this discovery by Skavanga Mining could be even larger than we suspected,' Sharif went on, pushing some documents across the table to the other two men.

'And I hear that Skavanga boasts three sisters who have become known as the Skavanga Diamonds, which in itself intrigues me,' the dangerous-looking Spaniard commented as he peeled a Valencia orange with a blade as sharp as a scalpel.

'I'll tell you what I know, Raffa,' the sheikh promised his friend, better known as Don Rafael de Leon, Duke of Cantalabria, a mountainous and very beautiful region of Spain.

Count Roman Quisvada also sat forward. Roman was an expert in diamonds, with laboratories that specialised in cutting and polishing high-value stones, while Raffa owned the world's largest and most exclusive chain of high-end retail jewellers. The Black Sheikh, the Italian count, and the Spanish duke had the diamond business sewn up.

There was just one loose end, Sharif reflected, and that was a company called Skavanga Mining. Owned by the three sisters, Britt, Eva and Leila Skavanga, along with the girls' absentee brother, Tyr, Skavanga Mining had reported the discovery of the largest diamond deposits ever recorded. He was on the point of going to Skavanga to check out these reports for himself.

While he was there he would check out Britt Skavanga, the oldest sister, who was currently running the company, Sharif mused as he drew a photograph towards him. She looked like a worthy opponent with her clear grey eyes, firm mouth and the tilt of that chin. He looked forward to meeting her. A deal with the added spice of down time in the bedroom held obvious appeal. There was no sentiment in business and he certainly wasted none on women.

'Why do you get all the fun?' Roman complained, frowning when Sharif told the other men about his plan.

'There are plenty to go round,' he reassured them dryly as the other two men studied the photographs of the sisters. Glancing at Raffa, he felt a momentary twinge of something close to apprehension. The youngest sister, whom Raffa was studying, was clearly an innocent, while Raffa was most certainly not.

'Three good-looking women,' Roman commented, glancing between his friends.

'For three ruthless asset strippers,' Raffa added, devouring the last piece of orange with relish. 'I look forward to stripping the assets off this one—'

Raffa's dark eyes blackened dangerously as Sharif gathered the photographs in. Sharif hardly realised that he was caressing the photograph of Britt Skavanga with his forefinger while denying Raffa further study of Leila, the youngest sister.

'This could be our most promising project to date,' the man known to the world as the Black Sheikh commented.

'And if anyone can land this deal, Sharif can,' Roman remarked, hoping to heal the momentary rift between his friends. He could only be thankful their interest wasn't in the same girl.

Raffa's laugh relaxed them all. 'Didn't I hear you have some interesting sexual techniques in Kareshi, Sharif? Silken ties? Chiffon blindfolds?'

Roman huffed a laugh at this. 'I've heard the same

thing. In the harem tents it's said they use creams and potions to send sensation through the roof—'

'Enough,' Sharif rapped, raising his hands to silence his friends. 'Can we please return to business?'

Within seconds the Skavanga girls were forgotten and the talk was all of balance sheets and financial predictions, but in one part of his mind Sharif was still thinking about a pair of cool grey eyes and a full, expressive mouth, and what could be accomplished with a little expert tutelage.

An absolute monarch, bred to a hard life in the desert, Sharif had been trained to rule and fight and argue at council with the wisest of men—women being notable by their absence, which was something he had changed as soon as he took over the country. Women in Kareshi had used to be regarded as ornaments to be pampered and spoiled and hidden away; under his rule they were expected to pull their weight. Education for all was now the law.

And who would dare to argue with the Black Sheikh? Not Britt Skavanga, that was for sure. Staring at Britt's photograph and seeing the steely determination so similar to his own in her eyes only reinforced his intention to check out all the assets in Skavanga personally. Britt possessed the generous, giving mouth of a concubine, with the unrelenting gaze of a Viking warrior. The combination aroused him. Even the severity of the suit she was wearing intrigued him. Her breasts thrusting against the soft wool stirred his senses in a most agreeable way. He adored severe tailoring on a woman. It was a type of shorthand he had learned to read many years ago. Severe equalled repressed, or possibly a player who liked to tease. Either way, he was a huge fan.

'Are you still with us, Sharif?' Raffa enquired with

amusement as his friend finally pushed Britt's photograph away.

'Yes, but not for long as I will be leaving for Skavanga in the morning, travelling in my capacity of geologist and advisor to the consortium. This will allow me to make an impartial assessment of the situation without ruffling any feathers.'

'That's sensible,' Raffa agreed. 'Talk of the Black Sheikh descending on a business would be enough to send anyone into a panic.'

'Have you ever *descended* on a tasty business prospect without devouring it?' Roman enquired, hiding his smile.

'The fact that this mysterious figure, conjured by the press and known to the world as the Black Sheikh, has never had a photograph published will surely be an advantage to you,' Raffa suggested.

'I reserve judgement until we meet again when I will be in a position to tell you if the claims that have been made about the Skavanga Diamonds are true,' Sharif said with a closing gesture.

'We can ask for no more than that,' his two friends agreed.

'Well, clearly, I must be the one to meet him,' Britt insisted as the three sisters sat round the interestingly shaped—if not very practical, thanks to the holes the designer had punched in it—blonde wood kitchen table in Britt's sleek, minimalist, barely lived-in penthouse.

'Clearly—why?' Britt's feisty middle sister, Eva, demanded. 'Who says you have the right to take the lead in this new venture? Shouldn't we all have a part in it? What about the equality you're always banging on about, Britt?'

'Britt has far more business experience than we have,' the youngest and most mild-mannered sister, Leila, pointed out. 'And that's a perfectly sensible reason for Britt to be the one to meet with him,' Leila added, sweeping anxious fingers through her tumbling blonde curls.

'Perfectly sensible?' Eva scoffed. 'Britt has experience in mining iron ore and copper. But diamonds?' Eva rolled her emerald eyes. 'You must agree the three of us are virgins where diamonds are concerned?'

And Eva was likely to remain a virgin in every sense if she kept on like this, Britt thought, fretting like a mother over her middle sister. Eva had been a glass-half-empty type of person for as long as Britt could remember and sadly there were no dashing Petruchios in Skavanga to prevent Eva from turning into a fully-fledged shrew. 'I'm going to deal with this—and with him,' she said firmly.

'You and the Black Sheikh?' Eva said scornfully. 'You might be a hotshot businesswoman here in Skavanga, but the sheikh's business interests are global—and he runs a country. What on earth makes you think you can take a man like that on?'

'I know my business,' Britt said calmly. 'I know our mine and I'll be factual. I'll be cool and I'll be reasoned.'

'Britt's very good at doing stuff like this without engaging her emotions,' Leila added.

'Really?' Eva mocked. 'Whether she can or not remains to be seen.'

'I won't let you down,' Britt promised, knowing her sisters' concerns both for her and for the business had prompted this row. 'I've handled difficult people in the past and I'm well prepared to meet the Black Sheikh. I realise I must handle him with kid gloves—'

'Nice.' Eva laughed.

Britt ignored this. 'We would be unwise to underestimate him,' she said. 'The ruler of Kareshi is known as the Black Sheikh for a very good reason—'

'Rape and pillage?' Eva suggested scathingly.

Britt held her tongue. 'Sheikh Sharif is one of the foremost geologists in the world.'

'It's a shame we couldn't find any photographs of him,' Leila mused.

'He's a geologist, not a film star,' Britt pointed out. 'And how many Arab rulers have you seen photographs of?'

'He's probably so ugly he'd break the camera,' Eva muttered. 'I bet he's a nerd with pebble glasses and a bristly chin.'

'If he is he would be easier for Britt to deal with,' Leila said hopefully.

'A ruler who has moved his country forward and brought peace sounds like a decent man to me, so, whatever he looks like, it doesn't matter. I just need your support. Fact: the minerals at the mine are running out and we need investment. The consortium this man heads up has the money to allow us to mine the diamonds.'

There was a silence as Britt's sisters accepted the truth of this and she breathed a sigh of relief when they nodded their heads. Now she had a chance to rescue the mine and the town of Skavanga that was built around it. That, together with all the fresh challenges ahead of her, made her meeting with the so-called Black Sheikh seem less of a problem.

She was feeling slightly less sanguine the following day.

'Serves you right for building up your hopes,' Eva said as the girls gathered in Britt's study after hearing her groan. 'Your famous Black Sheikh can't even be bothered to meet with you,' Eva remarked, peering over Britt's shoulder at the email message on the computer screen. 'So he's sending a representative instead,' she scoffed, turning to throw an I-told-you-so look at Leila.

'I'll get some fresh coffee,' Leila offered.

Eva's carping was really getting on Britt's nerves. She'd been up since dawn exchanging emails with Kareshi. It was practically noon for her, Britt reflected angrily as Leila brought the coffee in. Her sisters loved staying in the city with her, but sometimes they forgot that, while they could lounge around, she had a job to do. 'I'm still going to meet with him. What else am I going to do?' she demanded, swinging round to confront her sisters. 'Do you two have any better ideas?'

Eva fell silent, while Leila gave Britt a sympathetic look as she handed her a mug of coffee. 'I'm just sorry we're going back home and leaving you with all this to deal with.'

'That's my job,' Britt said, controlling her anger. She could never be angry with Leila. 'Of course I'm disappointed I won't be meeting the Black Sheikh, but all I've ever asked for is your support, Eva.'

'Sorry,' Eva muttered awkwardly. 'I know you got landed with the company when Mum and Dad died. I'm just worried about what's going to happen now all the commodities are running out. I do realise the mine's sunk without the diamonds. And I know you'll do your very best to land this deal, but I'm worried about you, Britt. This is too much on your shoulders.'

'Stop it,' Britt warned, giving her sister a hug. 'Whoever the Black Sheikh sends, I can deal with him.'

'It says that the man you're to expect is a qualified geologist,' Leila pointed out. 'So at least you'll have something in common.' Britt's degree was also in Geology, with a Master's in Business Management.

'Yes,' Eva agreed, trying to sound as optimistic as her sister. 'I'm sure it will be fine.'

Britt knew that both her sisters were genuinely concerned about her. They just had different ways of showing it. 'Well, I'm excited,' she said firmly to lift the mood. 'When this man gets here we're another step closer to saving the company.'

'I wish Tyr were here to help you.'

Leila's words made them all silent. Tyr was their long-lost brother and they rarely talked about him because it hurt too much. They couldn't understand why he had left in the first place, much less why Tyr had never contacted them.

Britt broke the silence first. 'Tyr would do exactly what we're doing. He thinks the same as us. He cares about the company and the people here.'

'Which explains why he stays away,' Eva murmured.

'He's still one of us,' Britt insisted. 'We stick together. Remember that. The discovery of diamonds might even encourage him to return home.'

'But Tyr isn't motivated by money,' Leila piped up.

Even Eva couldn't disagree with that. Tyr was an idealist, an adventurer. Their brother was many things, but money was not his god, though Britt wished he would come home again. She missed him. Tyr had been away too long.

'Here's something that will make you laugh,' Leila said in an attempt to lift the mood. Pulling the newspaper towards her, she pointed to an article in the newspaper that referred to the three sisters as the Skavanga Diamonds. 'They haven't tired of giving us that ridiculous nickname.'

'It's just so patronising,' Eva huffed, brushing a cascade of fiery red curls away from her face.

'I've been called worse things,' Britt argued calmly.

'Don't be so naïve,' Eva snapped. 'All that article does is wave a flag in front of the nose of every fortune-hunter out there—'

'And what's wrong with that?' Leila interrupted. 'I'd just like to see a man who isn't drunk by nine o'clock—'

This brought a shocked intake of breath from Britt and Eva, as Leila had mentioned something else they never spoke about. There had long been a rumour that their father had been drunk when he piloted the small company plane to disaster with their mother on board.

Leila flushed red as she realised her mistake. 'I'm sorry—I'm just tired of your sniping, Eva. We really should get behind Britt.'

'Leila's right,' Britt insisted. 'It's crucial we keep our focus and make this deal work. We certainly can't afford to fall out between us. That article is fluff and we shouldn't even be wasting time discussing it. If Skavanga Mining is going to have a future we have to consider every offer on the table—and so far the consortium's is the only offer.'

'I suppose you could always give the sheikh's representative a proper welcome, Skavanga style,' Eva suggested, brightening.

Leila relaxed into a smile. 'I'm sure Britt has got a few ideas up her sleeve.'

'It's not my sleeve you need to worry about,' Britt commented dryly, relieved that they were all the best of friends again.

'Just promise me you won't do anything you'll regret,' Leila said, remembering to worry.

'I won't regret it at the time,' Britt promised dryly.

'Unless he truly is a boffin with pebble glasses—in which case I'll just have to put a paper bag over his head.'

'Don't become overconfident,' Eva warned.

'I'm not worried. If he proves difficult I'll cut a hole in the ice and send him swimming. That will soon cool his ardour—'

'Why stop there?' Eva added. 'Don't forget the birch twig switches. You can always give him a good thrashing. That'll sort him out.'

'I'll certainly consider it—'

'Tell me you're joking?' Leila begged.

Thankfully, Britt's younger sister missed the look Britt and Eva exchanged.

CHAPTER TWO

BRITT WAS UNUSUALLY nervous. The breakfast meeting with the Black Sheikh's representative had been arranged for nine and it was already twenty past when she rushed through the doors of Skavanga Mining and tore up the stairs. It wasn't as if she was unused to business meetings, but this one was different for a number of reasons, not least of which was the fact that her car had blown a tyre on the way to the office. Changing a tyre was an energetic exercise at the best of times, enough to get her heart racing, but the circumstances of this meeting had made her anxious without that, because so much depended on it—

'I'll show myself in,' she said as a secretary glanced up in surprise.

Pausing outside the door to the boardroom, she took a moment to compose herself. Eva was right in that when their parents were killed Britt had been the only person qualified to take over the company and care for her two younger sisters. Their brother was… Well, Tyr was a maverick—a mercenary, for all they knew. He had been a regular soldier at one time, and no one knew where he was now. It was up to her to cut this deal; there was no one else. The man inside the boardroom could save the company if he gave a green light to the consortium.

And she was late, an embarrassment that put her firmly on the back foot.

Back foot?

Forget that, Britt concluded as the imposing figure standing silhouetted against the light by the window turned to face her. The man was dressed conventionally in a dark, beautifully tailored business suit, when somehow she had imagined her visitor would be wearing flowing robes. This man needed no props to appear exotic. His proud, dark face, the thick black hair, which he wore carelessly swept back, and his watchful eyes were all the exotic ingredients required to complete a stunning picture. Far from the bristly nerd, he was heart-stoppingly good-looking, and it took all she'd got to keep her feet marching steadily across the room towards him.

'Ms Skavanga?'

The deep, faintly accented voice ran shivers through every part of her. It was the voice of a master, a lover, a man who expected nothing less than to be obeyed.

Oh, get over it, Britt told herself impatiently. It was the voice of a man and he was tall, dark and handsome. So what? She had a company to run.

'Britt Skavanga,' she said firmly, advancing to meet him with her hand outstretched. 'I'm sorry, you have me at a disadvantage,' she added, explaining that all she had been told was that His Majesty Sheikh Sharif al Kareshi would be sending his most trusted aide.

'For these preliminary discussions that is correct,' he said, taking hold of her hand in a grip that was controlled yet deadly.

His touch stunned her. It might have been disappointingly brief, but it was as if it held some electrical charge that shot fire through her veins.

She wanted him.

Just like that she wanted him?

She was a highly sexed woman, but she had never experienced such an instant, strong attraction to any man before.

'So,' she said, lifting her chin as she made a determined effort to pitch her voice at a level suitable for the importance of the business to be carried out between them, 'what may I call you?'

'Emir,' he replied, more aloof than ever.

'Just Emir?' she said.

'It's enough.' He shrugged, discarding her wild fantasy about him at a stroke.

'Shall we make a start?' He looked her up and down with all the cool detachment of a buyer weighing up a mare brought to market. 'Have you had some sort of accident, Ms Skavanga?'

'Please, call me Britt.' She had completely forgotten about the tyre until he brought it up, and now all she could think was what a wreck she must look. She clearly wasn't making an impression as an on-top-of-things businesswoman, that was for sure.

'Would you like to take a moment?' Emir enquired as she smoothed her hair self-consciously.

'No, thank you,' she said, matching his cool. She wasn't about to hand over the initiative this early in the game. 'I've kept you waiting long enough. A tyre blew on my way to the office,' she explained.

'And *you* changed it?'

She frowned. 'Why wouldn't I? I didn't want to waste time changing my clothes.'

'Thank you for the consideration.' Emir dipped his head in a small bow, allowing her to admire his thick, wavy hair, though his ironic expression suggested that

Emir believed a woman's place was somewhere fragrant and sheltered where she could bake and quake until her hunter returned.

Was he married?

She glanced at his ring-free hands, and remembered to thank him when he pulled out a chair. She couldn't remember the last time that had happened. She was used to fending for herself, though it was nice to meet a gentleman, even if she suspected that beneath his velvet charm Emir was ruthless and would use every setback she experienced to his advantage.

No problem. She wasn't about to give him an inch.

'Please,' she said, indicating a place that put the wide expanse of the boardroom table between them.

He had the grace of a big cat, she registered as he sat down. Emir was dark and mysterious compared to the blond giants in Skavanga she was used to. He was big and exuded power like some soft-pawed predator.

She had to be on guard at all times or he would win this game before she even knew it had been lost. Business was all that mattered now—though it was hard to concentrate when the flow of energy between them had grown.

Chemistry, she mused. And no wonder when Emir radiated danger. The dark business suit moulded his athletic frame to perfection, while the crisp white shirt set off his bronzed skin, and a grey silk tie provided a reassuring sober touch—to those who might be fooled. She wasn't one of them. Emir might as well have been dressed in flowing robes with an unsheathed scimitar at his side, for seductive exoticism flowed from him.

She looked away quickly when his black gaze found hers and held it. *Damn!* She could feel her cheeks blazing. She quickly buried her attention in the documents in front of her.

Britt's apparent devotion to her work amused him. He'd felt the same spark between them that she had, and there was always the same outcome to that. He generally relied on the first few minutes of any meeting to assess people. Body language told him so much. Up to now Skavanga had not impressed him. It was a grey place with an air of dejection that permeated both the company and the town. He didn't need the report in front of him to tell him that the mineral deposits were running out, he could smell failure in the air. And however good this woman was at running the business—and she must be good to keep a failing company alive for so long—she couldn't sell thin air. Britt needed to mine those diamonds in order to keep her company alive, and to do that she needed the consortium he headed up to back her.

The town might be grey, but Britt Skavanga was anything but. She exceeded his expectations. There was a vivid private world behind those serious dove grey eyes, and it was a world he intended to enter as soon as he could.

'You will relate our dealings verbatim to His Majesty?' she said as they began the meeting.

'Of course. His Majesty greets you as a friend and hopes that all future dealings between us will bring mutual respect as well as great benefit to both our countries.'

He had not anticipated her sharp intake of breath, or the darkening of her eyes as he made the traditional Kareshi greeting, touching his chest, his mouth and finally his brow. He amended his original assessment of Britt to that of a simmering volcano waiting to explode.

She recovered quickly. 'Please tell His Majesty that I welcome his interest in Skavanga Mining, and may I also welcome you as his envoy.'

Nicely done. She was cool. He'd give her that. His senses roared as she held his gaze. The only woman he knew who would do that was his sister, Jasmina, and she was a troublesome minx.

As Britt continued to lay out her vision of the future for Skavanga Mining he thought there was a touching innocence about her, even in the way she thought she would have any say once the consortium took over. Her capable hands were neatly manicured, the nails short and unpainted, and she wore very little make-up. There was no artifice about her. What you saw was what you got with Britt Skavanga—except for the fire in her eyes, and he guessed very few had seen that blaze into an inferno.

'You must find the prospect of mining the icy wastes quite daunting after what you're used to in the desert,' she was saying.

He returned reluctantly to business. 'On the contrary. There is a lot in Skavanga that reminds me of the vastness and variety of my desert home. It is a variety only obvious to those who see it, of course.' As much as he wanted this new venture to go ahead, he wanted Britt Skavanga even more.

As hard as she tried to concentrate, her body was making it impossible to think, but then her body seemed tuned to Emir's. She even found herself leaning towards him, and had to make herself sit back. Even then his heat curled around her. His face was stern, *which she loved,* and his scent, spicy and warm, sandalwood, maybe, it was a reminder of the exotic world he came from. Her sisters had already teased her mercilessly about Kareshi supposedly being at the forefront of the erotic arts. She had pretended not to listen to such non-sense, especially when they insisted that the people of Kareshi had a potion they used to heighten sensation. But she'd heard them. And now she was wondering if anything they'd said could be true—

'Ms Skavanga?'

She jerked alert as Emir spoke her name. 'I beg your pardon. My mind was just—'

'Wandering? Or examining the facts?' he said with amusement.

'Yes—'

'Yes? Which is it?'

She couldn't even remember the question. The blood rush to her cheeks was furious and hot, while Emir just raised a brow and his mouth curved slightly.

'Are you ready to continue?' he said.

'Absolutely,' she confirmed, sitting up straight. She was mad for this man—crazy for him. No way could she think straight until the tension had been released.

'There are some amendments I want to discuss,' he said, frowning slightly as he glanced up at her.

She turned with relief to the documents in front of her.

'I need more time,' she said.

'Really?' Emir queried softly.

She swallowed deep when she saw the look in his eyes. 'I don't think we should rush anything—'

'I don't think we should close any doors, either.'

Were they still talking about business? Shaking her-self round, she explained that she wouldn't be making any decisions on behalf of the other shareholders yet.

'And I need to take samples from the mine before I

can involve the consortium in such a large investment,' Emir pointed out.

He only had to speak for alarm bells to go off in every part of her body, making it impossible to think about anything other than long, moonlit nights in the desert. Not once since taking over at Skavanga Mining had she ever been so distracted during a meeting. It didn't help that she had thought the Black Sheikh's trusted envoy would be some greybeard with a courtly air.

'Here is your copy of my projections,' she said, forcing her mind back to business before closing her file to signify the end of the meeting.

'I have my own projections, thank you.'

She bridled at that before reminding herself that just a murmur from the Black Sheikh could rock a government, and that his envoy was hardly going to be a pushover when it came to negotiations.

'Before we finish, there's just one here on the second page,' he said, leaning towards her.

'I see it,' she said, stiffening as she tried to close her mind to Emir's intoxicating scent. And those powerful hands...the suppleness in his fingers...the strength in his wrists...

He caught her staring and she started blushing again. This was ridiculous. She was acting like a teenager on her first date.

Exhaling shakily, she sat back in the chair determined to recover the situation, but Emir was on a roll.

'You seem to have missed something here,' he said, pointing to another paragraph.

She never missed anything. She was meticulous in all her business dealings. But sure enough, Emir had found one tiny thing she had overlooked.

'And this clause can go,' he said, removing it with a strike of his pen.

'Now, just a minute—' She stared aghast as Emir deconstructed her carefully drawn-up plan. 'No,' she said firmly. 'That clause does not go, and neither does anything else without further discussion, and this part of the meeting is over.'

He sat back in his chair as she stood up, which explained why she wasn't ready for him moving in front of her to stand in her way.

'You seem upset,' he said. 'And I don't want the first part of our meeting to end badly.'

'Bringing in investors is a big step for me to take—'

'Britt—'

Emir's touch on her skin was like an incendiary device, but the fact that his hand was on her arm at all was an outrage. 'Let me go,' she warned softly, but they both heard the shake in her voice. And surely Emir could feel her trembling beneath his touch. He must feel the heated awareness in her skin.

He murmured something in his own language. It might as well have been a spell. She turned to look at him, not keen to go anywhere suddenly.

'It seems to me we have a timing problem, Britt. But there is a solution, if you will allow me to take it?'

Emir's eyes were dark and amused. At first she thought she must have misunderstood him, but there was no mistake, and the solution he was proposing had been in her mind for some time. But surely no civilised businessman would be willing to enter into such a risky entanglement within an hour of meeting her?

As Emir's hand grazed her chin she moved into his embrace, allowing him to turn her face up to his. This was no meeting between business colleagues. This was a meeting between a man and woman who were hot for each other, and the man was a warrior of the desert.

Emir promised pleasure. He also promised a chance to forget, and, for however short a time, the prospect of that seemed preferable at this moment to doing battle endlessly on every front. How would it feel to have this big man hold her and bring her pleasure? She must have swayed towards him, for the next thing she knew he was holding her in front of him.

'Why, Britt,' he said with amusement. 'If I'd known how badly you wanted this I'm sure we could have arranged something before the meeting.'

Emir's blunt approach should have shocked her—annoyed her—but instead it made her want him all the more, and as he brushed her lips with his she found herself instantly hungry, instantly frantic, for more pressure, more intimacy, and for everything to happen fast.

But Emir was even more experienced than she had realised, and now he took pleasure in subjecting her to an agonising delay. As the clock ticked, the tension built and he held her stare with his knowing and faintly amused look. She guessed Emir knew everything about arousal, and could only hope it wouldn't be long before he decided she had suffered enough. She voiced a cry of relief when he cupped her face in his warm, slightly roughened hands, and another when her patience was rewarded by a kiss that began lightly and then brutally mimicked the act her body so desperately craved.

It was in no way subjugation by a powerful man, but the meeting of eager mates, a fierce coupling between two people who knew exactly what they wanted from each other, and as Emir pressed her back against the boardroom table and set about removing her clothes she gasped in triumph and began ripping at his.

He tossed her jacket aside. She loosened his tie and dragged it off, letting it drop onto the floor. As he ripped her blouse open she battled with the buttons on his shirt. She exclaimed with pleased surprise when he lifted her and she clung to him as he stripped off her tights and her briefs. Suddenly it was all about seeing who could rid themselves of any barriers first. She was mindless sensation—hot flesh brushing, touching, cleaving, in a tangle of limbs and hectic breathing, while Emir remained calm and strong, and certain. He felt so good beneath her hands…so very good—

Too good! You have never felt like this about a man before—

Danger! This man can change your life—

You won't walk away from this with a smile on your face—

Using sheer force of will, she closed off her annoying inner voice. She wanted this. She needed it. This was her every fantasy come true. Even now as Emir took time to protect them both she saw no reason not to follow her most basic instinct. Why shouldn't she? Emir was—

Emir was enormous. He was entirely built to scale. Was she ready for this?

He made her forget everything the moment he caressed her breasts. Moaning, she rested back and let him do what he wanted with her. Just this once she wanted to feel that she didn't have to lead or fight. Just this once she could be the woman she had always dreamed of being—the woman who was with a man who knew how to please her.

And I wonder what he thinks about you—

To hell with what he thinks about me, she raged silently.

To hell with you, don't you mean?

CHAPTER THREE

BRITT WAS BEAUTIFUL and willing and he had needs. Willing? She was a wild cat with a body that was strong and firm, yet voluptuous. Her breasts were incredible, uptilted and full, and he took his time to weigh them appreciatively, smiling when she groaned with pleasure as he circled her nipples very lightly with his thumbnails. She was so responsive, so eager that her nipples had tightened and were thrusting towards him, pink and impertinent, and clearly in need of more attention. He aimed to please. Kissing her neck, he travelled down, part of him already regretting that they had wasted so much time. She shuddered with desire as he blazed a trail through the dust she had collected when she changed her tyre. 'You're clean now,' he said, smiling into her lust-dazed eyes.

She laughed down low in her throat in a way he found really sexy, and then weakened against him as she waited for him to continue his sensory assault.

'Shall I take the edge off your hunger?' he offered.

'Yours too,' she insisted huskily.

'If that's what you want, you tell me what you'd like.'

Her gaze flicked up and her cheeks flushed pink. She wasn't sure whether to believe him or not.

'I'm serious,' he said quietly.

'Please—'

As she appealed to him he decided that the time he had allowed for this visit to Skavanga wouldn't be enough. He ran his fingers lightly over her beautiful breasts before moving on to trace the swell of her belly. Lifting her skirt, he nudged her thighs apart. She made it easy for him, so he repaid her gesture by delicately exploring the heated flesh at the apex of her thighs. When she whimpered with pleasure it was all he could do to hold back. So much for his much-vaunted self-control, he mused, as Britt thrust her hips towards him, trying for more contact. He wanted nothing more than to take her now. Clutching his arms, she tilted herself back against the table, moaning with need. Opening her legs a little more for him, she showed him a very different woman from the one in the starchy photograph he had examined in London, but this was the woman he had suspected Britt was hiding all along.

'You're quite clinical about this, aren't you?' Britt panted in a rare moment of lucidity as he watched her pleasure.

Duty could do that to a man. He never let himself go. Growing up the second son of the third wife had hardly been to his advantage as a youth. He had been forced to watch the cruelty inflicted on his people by those closer to the throne than he was on a daily basis. So, yes, he was cold. He'd had to be to overthrow tyrants that were also his relatives. There was no room now in his life for anything other than the most basic human appetite.

'Don't make me wait,' Britt was begging him.

She needn't worry. His preference at this moment was to please her.

This was insane. Emir was cold, detached—and the

sexiest thing on two legs. He was frighteningly distant, but she was lost in an erotic haze of his making. She needed more—more pressure, more contact—more of him. The more aloof he was, the more her body cried out to him. The ache he'd set up inside her was unbearable. She had to have more of his skilful touches—

An excited cry escaped her throat when she felt the insistent thrust of his erection against her belly. She rubbed herself shamelessly against it, sobbing with pleasure as each delicious contraction of her nerve endings gave some small indication of what was to come. Emir's hard, warrior frame was even more powerful than she had imagined, and yet he used his hands so delicately in a way that drove her crazy for him. Lacing her fingers through his thick black hair, she dragged him close. He responded by cupping the back of her head to keep her in place as he dipped down and plundered her mouth. Sweeping the table clear, he lifted her and balanced her on the edge. Moving between her legs, he forced them apart with the width of his body. 'Wrap your legs around me,' he commanded, pushing them wider still.

She had never obeyed a man's instructions in her life, but she rushed to obey these. Resting her hands flat on the table behind her, she arched her spine, thrusting her breasts forward, while Emir reared over her, magnificent and erect.

Like a stallion on the point of servicing a mare?

With far more consideration than that—

Are you sure?

She was sure that any more delay would send her crazy. She was also sure that Emir knew exactly what he was doing.

'Tell me what you want, Britt,' he demanded fiercely.

'You know what I want,' she said.

'But you must tell me,' he said in low, cruel voice.

Her throat dried. The harsher he got, the more arousing she found it. No one had ever pushed her boundaries like this before. And she had thought herself liberal where sex was concerned? She was a novice compared to Emir.

She had also thought herself emotion-free, Britt realised, but knew deep in her heart that something had changed inside her. Even when she plumbed the depths of Emir's cold black eyes she wanted to be the one to draw a response from him—she wanted to learn more about him, and in every way.

'Say it,' he instructed.

Her face blazed red. No one spoke to her like that—no one told her what to do. But her body liked what was happening, and was responding with enthusiasm. 'Yes,' she said. 'Yes, please.' And then she told him exactly what she wanted him to do to her without sparing a single lurid detail.

Now he was pleased. Now she got through to him. Now he almost smiled.

'I think I can manage that,' he said dryly. 'My only concern is that we may not have sufficient time to work our way through your rather extensive wish list.'

On this occasion, she thought. 'Perhaps another time,' she said, matching him for dispassion. But then she glanced at the door. How could she have forgotten that it was still unlocked? Just as she was thinking she must do something about it, Emir touched her in a way that made it impossible for her to move.

'Don't you like the risk?' he said, reading her easily.

She looked at him, and suddenly she loved the risk.

'Hold me,' he said softly. 'Use me—take what you need.'

She hesitated, another first for her. No one had ever given her this freedom. She moved to do as he said and found it took two hands to enclose him.

'I'm waiting,' he said.

With those dangerous eyes watching her, she made a pass. Loving it, she made a second, firmer stroke—

Taking control, Emir caught the tip inside her. She gasped and would have pulled away, but he cupped her buttocks firmly in his strong hands and drew her slowly on to him. 'What are you afraid of?' he said, staring deep into her eyes. 'You know I won't hurt you.'

She didn't know him at all, but for some reason she trusted him. 'I'm just—'

'Hungry,' he said. 'I know.'

A sound of sheer pleasure trembled from her throat. She had played games with boys before, she realised, but Emir was a man, and a man like no other man.

'Am I enough for you?' he mocked.

She lifted her chin. 'What do you think?'

He told her exactly what he thought, and while she was still gasping with shock and lust he kissed her, and before she could recover he thrust inside her deeply to the hilt. For a moment she was incapable of thinking or doing, and even breathing was suspended. This wasn't pleasure, this was an addiction. She could never get enough of this—or of him. The sensation of being completely inhabited while being played by a master was a very short road to release.

'No,' he said sharply, stopping her. 'I'll tell you when. Look at me, Britt,' he said fiercely.

On the promise of pleasure she stared into Emir's molten gaze. She would obey him. She would pay whatever price it took for this to continue.

He was pleased with her. Britt was more responsive

than even he had guessed. She was a strong woman who made him want to pleasure her. He loved the challenge that was Britt Skavanga. He loved her fire. He loved her cries of pleasure and the soft little whimpers she made when he thrust repeatedly into her. What had started as a basic function to clear his head had become an exercise in pleasuring Britt.

'Now,' he whispered fiercely.

He held her firmly as she rocked into orgasm with a release so violent he trusted his strength more than the boardroom table and held her close, though he could do nothing about the noise she was making, which would probably travel to the next town, and so he smothered it with a kiss. When he let her go, she gasped and called his name. He held her safe, cushioning her against the hard edge of the table with his hands as he soothed her down. Withdrawing carefully, he steadied Britt on her feet before releasing her. Smoothing the hair back from her flushed, damp brow, he stared into her dazed eyes, waiting until he was sure she had recovered. The one thing he had not expected was to feel an ache of longing in his chest. He had not expected to feel anything.

'Wow,' she whispered, her voice muffled against his naked chest.

He liked the feeling of Britt resting on him and was in no hurry to move away. If she had been anyone else the next move would have been simple. He would have taken her back to Kareshi with him. But she was too much like him. There would be no diamond mine, no town, no Skavanga Mining, without Britt. Just as he belonged in Kareshi, she was tied here. But still he felt a stab of regret that he couldn't have this exciting woman. 'Are you okay?' he murmured as she stirred.

She lifted her chin to look at him, and as she did this

she drew herself up and drew her emotions in. As she pulled herself together he could almost see her forcing herself to get over whatever it was she had briefly felt for him.

'There are two bathrooms,' she informed him briskly. 'You can use the one directly off the boardroom. I have my own en suite attached to my office. We will reconvene this meeting in fifteen minutes.'

A smile of incredulity and, yes, admiration curved his lips as he watched her go. She walked across the room with her head held high like a queen. It might have seemed ridiculous had anyone else tried it, but Britt Skavanga could pull it off.

He showered down quickly in the bathroom she had told him about, and was both surprised and pleased by the quality of the amenities until he remembered that Britt had a hand in everything here. There were high-quality towels on heated rails, as well as shampoo, along with all the bits and pieces that contributed to making a freshen-up session pleasurable. Britt hadn't forgotten anything—at which point a bolt of very masculine suspicion punched him in the guts. Had she done this before? And if so, how many times?

And why should he care?

He returned to the boardroom to find Britt had arrived before him. She looked composed. She looked as if nothing had happened between them. She looked as she might have looked at the start of the meeting if she hadn't been forced to change a tyre first. She also looked very alone to him, seated beneath the portraits of her forebears, and once again he got the strongest sense that duty ruled Britt every bit as much as it ruled him.

They both imagined they were privileged and, yes, each was powerful in their own way, but neither of them could choose what they wanted out of life, because the choices had already been made for them.

She hated herself, *hated herself* for what she had done. Losing control like that. She hadn't even been able to meet her sex-sated reflection in the bathroom mirror. She had weakened with Emir in a way she must never weaken again. She put it down to a moment of madness before she closed her heart. But as her mind flashed back to what they'd done, and the remembered feeling of being close to him, for however short a time, she desperately wanted more—

She would just have to exercise more control—

'Is something distracting you, Britt?' Emir demanded, jolting her back to the present.

'Should there be something?' she said in a voice that held no hint that Emir was the only distraction.

'No,' he said without expression.

They deserved each other, she thought. But she was curious all the same. Did he really feel nothing? Didn't his body throb with pleasurable awareness as hers did? Didn't he want more? Didn't he yearn to know more about her as she longed to know more about him? Or was she nothing more than an entertainment between coffee breaks for Emir?

And rumour had it she was the hardest of the Skavanga Diamonds?

What a laugh!

Tears of shame were pricking her eyes. She could never make a mistake like this again—

'Hay fever,' she explained briskly when Emir glanced suspiciously at her.

'In Skavanga?' he said, glancing outside at the icy scene.

'We have pollen,' she said coldly, moving on.

She wasn't sure how she got to the end of the second half of their meeting, but she did. There was too much hanging on the outcome for her to spoil the deal with a clouded mind. So far so good, Britt concluded, wrapping everything up with a carefully rehearsed closing statement. At least she could tell her sisters that she hadn't been forced to concede anything vital, and that Emir was prepared to move on to the next stage, which would involve a visit to the mine.

'I'm looking forward to that,' he said.

There was nothing in his eyes for her. The rest of Emir's visit would be purely about business—

And why should it be anything else?

She hated herself for the weakness, but she had expected something—some outward sign that their passionate encounter had made an impression on him... but apparently not.

'Is that everything?' Emir said as he gathered up his papers. 'I imagine you want to make an early start in the morning if we're going to the mine.'

The mine was miles away from anywhere. The only logical place for them to stay was the old cabin Britt's great-grandfather had built. It was isolated—there were no other people around. Doing a quick risk-assessment of the likely outcome, knowing the passion they shared, she knew she would be far better off arranging for one of her lieutenants to take him...

But Emir would see that as cowardice. And was she frightened of him? Could she even entrust the task of taking him to the mine to anyone else? She should be there. And maybe getting him out of her system once and for all would allow her to sharpen up and concentrate on what really mattered again.

'I would like to make an early start,' she said, 'though I must warn you there are no luxury facilities at the cabin. It's pretty basic.' Somehow, what Emir thought about the cabin that meant so much to her mattered to her, Britt realised. It mattered a lot.

Emir seemed unconcerned. 'Apart from the difference in temperature, the Arctic is another wilderness like the desert.'

'My great-grandfather built the cabin. It's very old–'

'You're fortunate to have something so special and permanent to remember him by.'

Yes, she was, and the fact that Emir knew this meant a lot to her.

They stared at each other until she forced herself to look away. This was not the time to be inventing imaginary bonds between them. Better she remembered Eva's words about a true Nordic welcome to contain this warrior of the desert. It would be interesting to discover if Emir was still so confident after a brush with ice and fire.

CHAPTER FOUR

HE LEARNED MORE about Britt during the first few hours of their expedition than he had learned in any of the reports. She was intelligent and organised, energetic and could be mischievous, which reminded him to remain on guard.

She had called him at five-thirty a.m.—just to check he was awake, she had assured him. He suspected he hadn't slept after their encounter, and guessed she was hoping he'd had a sleepless night too. He gave nothing away.

It couldn't strictly be called dawn when her Jeep rolled up outside his hotel, since at this time of year in Skavanga a weak grey light washed the land for a full twenty-four hours. Only Britt coloured the darkness when she sprang down and came to greet him. He was waiting for her just outside the doors. Her hair gleamed like freshly harvested wheat and she had pulled an ice-blue beanie over her ears to protect them from the bitter cold. Her cheeks and lips were whipped red by the harshest of winds, and she was wearing black polar trousers tucked into boots, with a red waterproof jacket zippered up to her neck. She looked fresh and clean and bright, and determined.

'Britt—'

'Emir.'

Her greeting was cool. His was no more than polite, though he noticed that the tip of her nose was as red as her full bottom lip and her blue-grey eyes were the colour of polar ice. She gave him the once-over, and seemed satisfied by what she saw. He knew the drill. He might live in the desert, but he was no stranger to Arctic conditions.

'Was the hotel okay?' she asked him politely when they were both buckled in.

'Yes. Thank you,' he said, allowing his gaze to linger on her face

She shot him a glance and her cheeks flushed red. She was remembering their time in the boardroom. He was too.

She drove smoothly and fast along treacherous roads and only slowed for moose and for a streak of red fox until they entered what appeared to be an uninhabited zone. Here the featureless ice road was shielded on either side between towering walls of packed snow. She still drove at a steady seventy and refused his offer to take over. She knew the way, she said. She liked to be in control, he thought. Except when she was having sex when she liked him to take the lead.

'We'll soon be there,' she said, distracting him from these thoughts.

They had been climbing up the side of a mountain for some time, leaving the ice walls far behind. Below them was a vast expanse of frozen lake—grey, naturally.

'The mine is just down there,' she said when he craned his neck to look.

He wondered what other delights awaited him. All he could be sure of was that Britt hadn't finished with him yet. She liked to prove herself, so he was confident the test would include some physical activity. He looked forward to it, just as he looked forward to a return bout with her in the desert.

Emir seemed utterly relaxed and completely at home in a landscape that had terrified many people she had brought here. She knew this place like the back of her hand, and yet, truthfully, had never felt completely safe. Knowing Emir, he had probably trialled every extreme sport known to man, so what was a little snow and ice to him?

'Penny for them,' he said.

She made herself relax so she could clear her mind and equivocate. 'I'm thinking about food. Aren't you?'

She was curious to know what he was thinking, but as usual Emir gave nothing away.

'Some,' he murmured.

She glanced his way and felt her heart bounce. She would never get used to the way he looked, and for one spark of interest from those deceptively sleepy eyes she would happily walk barefoot in the snow, which was something Emir definitely didn't need to know.

'The food's really good at the mine,' she said, clinging to safe ground. 'And the catering staff will have stocked the cabin for us. The food has to be excellent when people are so isolated. It's one of the few pleasures they have.'

'I wouldn't be too sure about that,' he said dryly.

'There are separate quarters for men and women,' she countered promptly—and primly.

'Right.' His tone was sceptical.

'You seem to know a lot about it,' she said, feeling a bit peeved—jealous, maybe, especially when he said,

'It's much the same for people who work in the desert.'

'Oh, I see.'

'Good,' he said, ignoring her sharp tone and settling back. 'I'm going to doze now, if you don't mind?'

'Not at all.'

Sleep? Yeah, right—like a black panther sleeps with one eye open. There was no such thing as stand down for Emir.

Emir could play her at her own game, and play it well, Britt realised as she turned off the main road. She could be cool, but he would be cooler, and now there was no real contact between them as he dozed—apparently—which she regretted. He wanted her to feel this way—to feel this lack of him, she suspected.

'Sorry,' she exclaimed with shock as the Jeep lurched on the rutted forest track. The moment's inattention had jolted Emir awake and had almost thrown them into the ditch.

'No problem,' he said. 'If you want me to drive...?'

'I'm fine. Thank you.' She'd heard that the ruler of Kareshi was introducing change, but not fast enough, clearly. Emir probably resented her running the company too. He came from a land where men ruled and women obeyed—

She gasped as his hand covered hers. 'Take it easy,' he said, steadying the steering wheel as it bounced in her hands.

'I've been travelling these roads since I was a child.'

'Then I'm surprised you don't know about the hazards of melting snow.'

He definitely deserved a session in the sauna and a dip in the freezing lake afterwards, she concluded.

'We're nearly there,' she said.

'Good.'

Why the smile in his voice? Was he looking forward to their stay at the isolated cabin? She squirmed in her seat at the thought that he might be and then wondered angrily why she was acting this way. It was one thing bringing her city friends into the wilderness for a rustic weekend, but quite another bringing Emir down here when there could only be one outcome—

Unless he had had enough of her, of course, but something told her that wasn't the case. She'd stick with her decision to enjoy him and get him out of her system, Britt concluded, explaining that the nearest hotel was too far away from the mine to stay there.

'You don't have to explain to me, Britt. I like it here. You forget,' Emir murmured as she drew to a halt outside the ancient log cabin, 'the wilderness is my home.'

And now she was angry with him for being so pleased with everything. And even angrier with herself because Emir was right, the wilderness was beautiful in its own unique way, she thought, staring out across the glassy lake. It was as if she were seeing it for the first time. Because she was seeing it through Emir's eyes, Britt realised, and he sharpened her focus on everything.

'This is magnificent,' he exclaimed as they climbed down from the Jeep.

She tensed as he came to stand beside her. Her heart pumped and her blood raced as she tried not to notice how hot he looked in the dark, heavy jacket and snow boots. Emir radiated something more than the confidence of a man who was sensibly dressed and comfortable in this extreme temperature. He exuded the type of strength that anyone would like to cling to in a storm—

He looked downright dangerous, she told herself sensibly, putting a few healthy feet of fresh air between them. But the lake was beautiful, and neither of them was in any hurry to move away. It stretched for miles and was framed by towering mountains whose jagged peaks were lost in cloud. A thick pine forest crept up these craggy slopes until there was nothing for the roots to cling to. But it was the silence that was most impressive, and that was heavy and complete. It felt almost as if the world were holding its breath, though she had to smile when Emir turned to look at the cabin and an eagle called.

'I'll grab our bags,' he said.

As he brushed past her on his way to the Jeep she shivered with awareness, and then smiled as she walked towards the cabin. She was always happy here—always in control. There would be no problems here. She'd keep things light and professional. Here, she could put what had happened between them in the boardroom behind her.

Emir caught up with her at the door, and his first question was how far was it to the mine? With her back to him, she pulled a wry face. Putting what had happened behind her was going to be easier than she had thought. They hadn't even crossed the threshold yet and Emir's mind was already set on business.

Which was exactly what she had hoped for—

Was it?

Of course it was, but she wasn't going to pretend it didn't sting. Everyone had their pride, and everyone wanted to feel special—

Hard luck for her, she thought ruefully.

'So, how far exactly is it to the mine?' he said. 'How long will it take by road?'

'Depending on the weather?' She turned the key in the lock. 'I'd say around ten minutes.'

'Is there any chance we can take a look around today, in that case?' Emir asked as he held the door for her.

He was in more of a hurry than she'd thought. Well, that was fine with her. She could accommodate a fast turnaround. 'The mine is a twenty-four-hour concern. We can visit as soon as you're ready.'

'Then I'd like to freshen up and go see it right away—if that's okay with you?'

'That's fine with me.' She had to stop herself laughing at the thought that she had never met anyone quite so much like her before.

As she used to be, Britt amended, before Emir came into her life. Taking charge of her bag, she hoisted it onto her shoulders. 'Welcome,' she said, walking into the cabin.

'This is nice,' Emir commented as he gazed around.

He made everything seem small, she thought, but in a good way. The cabin had been built by a big man for big men, yet could be described as cosy. On a modest scale, it still reflected the personality of the man who had built it and who had founded the Skavanga dynasty. With nothing but his determination, Britt's great-grandfather had practically clawed the first minerals out of the ground with his bare hands, and with makeshift tools that other prospectors had thrown away. There was nothing to be ashamed of here in the cabin. It was only possible to feel proud.

'What?' Emir said when he caught her staring at him.

'You're the only man apart from my brother who makes me feel small,' she said, managing not to make it sound like a compliment.

'I take it you're talking about your brother, Tyr?'

'My long-lost brother, Tyr,' she admitted with a shrug.

'I can assure you the very last thing on my mind is to make you feel small.'

'You don't—well, not in the way you mean. How tall are you, anyway?'

'Tall enough.'

She could vouch for that. And was that a glint of humour in Emir's eyes? Maybe this wouldn't be so bad, after all. Maybe bringing him to the cabin wasn't the worst idea she'd ever had. Maybe they could actually do business with each other *and* have fun.

And then say goodbye?

Why not?

'Are you going to show me to my room?' Emir prompted, glancing towards the wooden staircase.

'Yes, of course. '

Ditching her bag, she mounted the wooden stairs ahead of him, showing Emir into a comfortable double bedroom with a bathroom attached. 'You'll sleep in here,' she said. 'There are plenty of towels in the bathroom, and endless hot water, so don't stint yourself—and just give me a shout if you need anything more.'

'This is excellent,' he called downstairs to her. 'Thank you for putting me up.'

'As an alternative to having you camp down the mine?' She laughed. 'Of course, there are bunkhouses you could use—'

'I'm fine here.'

And looking forward to tasting some genuine Nordic hospitality, she hoped, tongue in cheek, as she glanced out of the window at the snow-clad scene.

'Britt—'

'What?' Heart pounding, she turned. Even now with all the telling off she'd given herself at the tempting thought of testing out the bed springs, she hoped and smiled and waited.

'Window keys?' Emir was standing on the landing, staring down at her. 'It's steaming hot in here.'

Ah… 'Sorry.'

She stood for a moment to compose herself and then ran upstairs to sort him out. The central heating she'd had installed was always turned up full blast before a visit. She could operate it from her phone, and thoughts of turning it down a little had flown out of the window along with her sensible head thanks to Emir. 'I suggest you leave the window open until the room cools down.' Fighting off all feelings about the big, hard, desirable body so very close to her, she unlocked the window and showed him where to hang the key.

'This is a beautiful room, Britt.'

The room was well furnished with a thick feather duvet on the bed, sturdy furniture, and plenty of throws for extra warmth. She'd hung curtains in rich autumnal shades to complement the wooden walls. 'Glad you think so.'

Now she had to look at him, but she lost no time making for the door.

'Are these your grandparents?'

She did not want to turn around, but how could she ignore the question when Emir was examining some sepia photographs hanging on the wall?

'This one is my great-grandfather,' she said, coming to stand beside him. The photographs had been hung on the wall to remind each successive generation of the legacy they had inherited. Her great-grandfather was a handsome, middle-aged man with a moustache and a big, worn hat. He was dressed in leather boots with his heavy trousers tucked into them, his hands were gnarled and he wore a rugged jacket, which was patched at the elbows. Even the pose, the way he was leaning on a spade, spoke volumes about those early days. Family and Skavanga Mining meant everything to her, Britt realised as she turned to leave the room.

She had to ask Emir to move. Why was he leaning against the door? "Excuse me…'

Straightening up, he moved aside. Now she was disappointed because he hadn't tried to stop her. What was wrong with her? She had brought a man she was fiercely attracted to to an isolated cabin. What did she think was going to happen? But now she wondered if sex with Emir would get him out of her system. Would anything?

At the top of the stairs she couldn't resist turning to see if he was still watching her.

Something else for her to regret. And what did that amused look signify—the bed was just a few tempting steps away?

And now the familiar ache had started up again. They were consenting adults who made their own agenda, and, with the mine open twenty-four seven, it wasn't as if they didn't have time—

And if she gave in to her appetite, Emir would expect everything to be on his terms from hereon in—

'I'll take quick a shower and see you outside in ten,' she called, running up the next flight of stairs to her own room in the attic. Slamming the door, she rested back against it. Saying yes to Emir would be the easiest thing in the world. Saying no to him required cast-iron discipline, and she wasn't quite sure she'd got that.

She had to have it, Britt told herself sternly as she showered down. Anything else was weakness.

Britt's bedroom was one of three at the cabin. She

had chosen it as a child, because she could be alone up here. She had always loved the pitched roof with its wealth of beams, thinking it was like something out of a fairy tale. When she was little she could see the sky and the mountains if she stood on the bed, and when she was on her own she could be anyone she wanted to be. Over the years she had collected items that made her feel good. Her grandmother had worked the patchwork quilt. Her grandfather had carved the headboard. These family treasures meant the world to her. They were far more precious than any diamonds, but then she had to remember the good the diamonds could do—for Skavanga, the town her ancestors had built, and for her sisters, and for the company.

She had to secure Emir's recommendation to his master, the Black Sheikh, Britt reflected as she toyed with some trinkets on the dressing table. They were the same cheap hair ornaments she had worn as a girl, she realised, picking them up and holding them against her long blonde hair so she could study the effect in the mirror. She hadn't even changed the threadbare stool in front of the dressing table, because her grandmother had worked the stitches, and because it was a reminder of the girl Britt had been, like the books by her bedside. This was a very different place from her penthouse in the centre of Skavanga, but the penthouse was her public face while this was where she kept her heart.

And to keep it she must cut that deal to her advantage—

With a man as shrewd as Emir in the frame?

She had never doubted her own abilities before, Britt realised as she wandered over to a window she could see out of now without standing on the bed. Skavanga

Mining had meant everything to her parents, but they hadn't been able to keep it—

Because her father was a drunk—

She shook her head, shaking out the memory. Her parents had tried their best—

Leaving little time for Britt and her siblings.

So she had picked up a mess. Lots of people had to do that. And somehow she would find a way to cut a favourable deal with the consortium.

Staring out of the window drew her gaze to the traditional sauna hut, sitting squat on the shore of the lake. With its deep hat of snow and rows of birch twigs switches hanging in a rack outside the door, it brought a smile to her face as she remembered Eva's teasing recommendation—that she bring Emir into line here. There were certainly several ways she could think of to do that. If only there weren't a risk he might enjoy them too much...

Seeing Emir's shadow darkening the snow outside, she quickly stepped back from the window. Tossing the towel aside, she pulled out the drawers of the old wooden chest and picked out warm, lightweight Arctic clothing—thermals, sweater, waterproof trousers and thick, sealskin socks. She resented the way her heart was drumming, as if she were going out on a date, rather than showing a man around a mine so he could make vast sums of money for his master out of generations of her family's hard work. She also hated the fact that Emir had beaten her to it downstairs. She was endlessly competitive. Having two sisters, she supposed. Determined to seize back the initiative, she knocked on the window to capture his attention, and when she'd got his attention she held up five fingers to let him know she'd be down right away. Almost. She'd brush her hair and put some lip gloss on first.

Traitor.

Everyone likes to feel good, Britt argued firmly with her inner voice. This has nothing to do with Sharif.

He had the cabin keys as well as the keys to the Jeep, and was settled behind the wheel by the time Britt appeared at the door. Climbing out, he strolled over to lock the cabin. She held out her hand to take charge of the keys.

'I'll keep them,' he said, stowing them in the pocket of his lightweight polar fleece.

Britt's crystal gaze turned stony.

'I'm driving too,' he said, enjoying the light floral scent she was wearing, which seemed at complete odds with the warrior woman expression on her face.

She was still seething when she swung into the passenger seat at his side. 'I know where we're going,' she pointed out.

'Then you can guide me there,' he said, gunning the engine. 'I'll turn the Sat Nav off.'

She all but growled at this.

'Why don't you let me drive?' she said.

'Why don't you direct me?' he said mildly, releasing the brake. 'It doesn't hurt to share the load from time to time,' he added, which earned him an angry glance.

They drove on in silence down the tree-shrouded lane. He noticed she glanced at the sauna on the lakeside as they drove past. He guessed his trials might begin there. The sauna was all ready and fired up. She wasn't joking when she'd said the people at the mine looked after her. The consortium would have to work hard to win hearts and minds as well as everything else if they were going to make this project a success. Perhaps they needed Britt's participation in the scheme more than he'd thought at first.

The snow was banked high either side of the road. The tall pines were bowed under its weight. The air was frigid with an icy mist overhanging everything. Snow was falling more heavily by the time they reached the main road. It had blurred the tyre tracks behind them and kept the windscreen wipers working frantically. 'Left or right?' he said, slowing the vehicle.

'If you'd let me drive—'

He put the handbrake on.

'Left,' she said impatiently.

As he swung the wheel Britt tugged off her soft blue beanie and her golden hair cascaded down. If she had been trying to win his attention she couldn't have thought up a better ruse, he realised as the scent of clean hair and lightly fragranced shampoo hit him square in the groin. He smiled to himself when she tied it back severely as if she knew that he liked it falling free around her shoulders. The fact that Britt didn't want to flaunt her femininity in front of him told him something. She liked him and she didn't want him to know.

'You must be tired,' he said, turning his thoughts to the stress she was under. It wasn't easy trying to salvage the family business, as he knew only too well. Whether it was a town or a country made no difference when people you cared about were involved. Her thoughts were with all the people who depended on her, as his were with Kareshi.

'I'm not as fragile as you seem to think,' she said, turning a hostile back on him as she stared out of the window.

She wasn't fragile at all. And if Britt tired at any

point, he'd be there. Crazy, but somehow this woman had got under his skin—and he had more than enough energy for both of them.

CHAPTER FIVE

EMIR HAD WHAT was needed to take the mine to the next level summed up within the first half hour of him visiting the immense open-cast site. Digging down into the Arctic core would require mega-machines, as well as an extension to the ice road in order to accommodate them, and that would take colossal funding.

With such vast sums involved he would oversee everything. Second in command—second in anything—wasn't his way. Britt was beginning to wonder how Emir managed to work for the sheikh—until he handed over the car keys.

As she thanked him she couldn't have been more surprised and wondered if she had earned some respect down the mine? She had known the majority of the miners most of her life, and got on with everyone, and, though her brother Tyr would have been their first choice, she knew that in Tyr's absence the miners respected her for taking on the job. Some of them had worked side by side with her grandfather, and she was proud to call them friends. She would do anything to keep them in employment.

Emir broke the silence as she started the engine. 'Once I've had the samples tested, we can start planning the work schedule in earnest.'

'I'm sure you won't be disappointed with the result of the test. I've had reports from some of the best brains in Europe, who all came to the same conclusion. The Skavanga mine is set to become the richest diamond discovery ever made.' If they could afford to mine the gems, she added silently. But surely now Emir had seen the mine for himself he wouldn't pull back. *He mustn't pull back.*

She tensed as he stretched out his long legs and settled back. 'So what do you think of the mine now you've seen it? Will you put in a good report? I have had other offers,' she bluffed in an effort to prompt him.

'If you've had other offers you must consider them all.'

Emir had called her bluff and left her hanging. Who else did he think could afford to do the work? It was the consortium or nothing. 'I would have liked Tyr to be involved, but we haven't seen him for years.'

'That doesn't mean he isn't around.'

'I'll have a word with our lawyers when we get back—to see if they can find him. I imagine you'll need to consult with your principal before making the next move?' She glanced across, but the only fallout from this was a heart-crunching smile from Emir. She turned up the heating, but there was ice in her blood. The fact remained that only three men had the resources to bring the diamonds to the surface.

'Why don't you stop by the sauna?' Emir suggested as she shivered involuntarily.

She was shivering, but at the thought of all the battles ahead of her.

Battles she hadn't looked for in a job she didn't want—

No one must know that. No one would *ever* know

that. She had accepted responsibility for the mine because there was no one else to do so, and had no intention of welching on that responsibility now. 'The sauna sounds like a good idea. I'm sure you'll enjoy it—'

'I'm sure I will too.'

It would be interesting to see if Emir felt quite so confident by the time they left the sauna.

Shock at the sudden dramatic change in temperature as they climbed out of the Jeep rendered them both silent for a few moments. The sky was uniform grey, though the Northern Lights had just begun to sweep across the bowl of the heavens as if a band of giants were waving luminescent flags. It was startling and awe-inspiring and they both lifted their heads to stare. The air was frigid, and mist formed in front of their mouths as they stood motionless as the display undulated above them.

The ice hole was probably frozen solid, Britt realised as the cold finally prompted them to move. They kept a power saw at the hut and that would soon sort it out. The sauna hut looked like a gingerbread house with a thick white coat of snow. It was another of her special places. Taking a sauna was a tradition she loved. It was the only way to thaw out the bones in Skavanga. And it was a great leveller as everyone stripped to the buff.

'No changing rooms?' Emir queried.

'Not even a shower,' she said, wondering if he was having second thoughts. 'We'll bathe in the lake afterwards.'

'Fine by me,' he said, gazing out across the glassy skating rink the lake had become.

As his lips pressed down with approval her attention was drawn to his sexy mouth. There wasn't much about Emir that wasn't sexy, and she couldn't pretend that she wasn't looking forward to seeing him naked. So far their encounters had been rushed, but there was no rushing involved in a traditional sauna. There would be all the time in the world to admire him.

She left him to open the locked compartment where the power saw was kept, but Emir wasn't too happy when she started it up. She turned, ready to give him a lecture on the fact that she had been cutting holes in the ice since she was thirteen, and stalled. That man could take his clothes off faster than anyone she knew. And could cause a ton of trouble just by standing there. How was she supposed to keep her gaze glued to his face?

'I'll cut the ice. You go inside. The sauna's been lit for some time. It should be perfect. Just ladle some more water on the hot stones—'

She hardly needed steam at this point, Britt reflected as Emir pushed through the door and disappeared. He was a towering monument to masculinity.

And she was going to share some down time with him?

She'd always managed to do so before with people without leaping on top of them—

And they all looked like Emir?

None of them looked like Emir.

Having cut the hole in the ice, she stripped down ready for the sauna. She kept her underwear on. She'd never done that before. Not that it offered much protection, but she felt better. And maybe it sent a message. If not, too bad; for the first time she could remember ever, she felt self-conscious, so the scraps of lace helped her, if no one else.

She found Emir leaning back on the wooden bench, perfectly relaxed, and perfectly naked as he allowed the steam rising from the hot stones on the brazier to roll over him.

She sat down in the shadows away from him, but couldn't settle.

'Too hot?' he asked as she constantly changed position.

Try, overheating…

And that was something else he didn't need to know. Emir's eyes might be closed, but she suspected he knew everything going on around him. If she needed proof of that, his faint smile told her everything. And as if she needed any more provocation with those hard-muscled legs stretched out in front of him, and his best bits prominently displayed—should she be foolish enough to take a look. She transferred her gaze to his face. His eyelashes were so thick and black they threw crescent shadows across his cheekbones, while his ebony brows swept up like some wild Tartar from the plains of Russia…

Or a sheikh…

Waves of shock and faintness washed over her, until she told herself firmly to give that overactive imagination of hers a rest. 'I'm going outside to cool off.'

Emir went as far as opening one eye.

'I'm going for a swim in the swimming hole—'

'Then I'm coming with you—'

'No need,' she said quickly, needing space.

Too late. Emir was already standing and taking up every spare inch in the hut. Regret at her foolishness replaced the shock and faintness. They should have said goodbye in Skavanga. She could have sent a trusted employee to the mine.

Could you trust anyone else to do this deal but you?

Whatever. There had to be an easier way than this.

'You can't go swimming in an ice lake on your own,' Emir said firmly, as if reading her.

'I've been swimming in the lake since I was a child.'

'When you were supervised, I imagine.'

'I'm old enough to take care of myself now.'

'Really?'

Emir's mockery was getting to her. And what did he think he was looking at now?

Oh... She quickly crossed her arms over her chest.

'I'm coming anyway,' he said, still with a flare of amusement in his eyes.

So be it, she thought, firming her jaw. In fairness, the golden rule at the cabin was that no one *ever* went swimming in the frozen lake alone. But did Emir have to tower over her to make his point?

He grabbed a towel on his way out, which he flung around her shoulders. 'You'll need it afterwards,' he said.

She gave him a look that said she didn't need his help, especially not here, and then gritted her teeth as she thought about the icy shock to come.

Running to the lake, she tossed her towel away at the last minute and jumped in before she had chance to change her mind.

She might have screamed. Who knew what she did or said? Once the icy water claimed her, rational thought was impossible. She was in shock and knew better than to linger. She was soon clambering out again—only to find Emir standing waiting for her with a towel.

'You didn't need to do that.'

He tossed the towel her way without another word, and then dived into the lake before she could stop him. She ran to the edge, but there was no sign of him— just loose ice floating. Panic consumed her, but just as she was preparing to jump in after him he emerged. Laughing.

Laughing!

Emir had barely cracked a smile the whole time he'd been in Skavanga, and *now* he was laughing?

She repaid the favour by tossing him a clean towel, which he wrapped around his waist. She didn't wait to see how securely he fixed it. She just pelted for the sauna and dived in. Emir was close behind and shut the door.

'Amazing,' he said, like a tiger that, finding itself in the Arctic, had played with polar bears and found it fun.

He shook his head, sending tiny rainbow droplets of glacier flying around the cabin like the diamonds they were both seeking.

'You enjoyed it, I see?' she said as the spray from him hissed on the hot stones.

'Of course I enjoyed it,' he exclaimed. 'I can think of only one thing better—'

She could be excused for holding her breath.

'Next you rub me down with ice—'

Before it melted? She doubted that was possible.

'I definitely want more,' he said, glancing through the window.

Oh, to be a frozen lake, she thought.

As Emir settled back on the wooden bench and closed his eyes she realised she was glad he had embraced her traditions, which led on naturally to wondering about his. She had to stop that before her thoughts took a turn for the seriously erotic.

'You love this place, don't you?' he said.

'It means a lot to me,' she admitted, 'as does the cabin.'

'It's what it represents,' Emir observed.

Correct, she thought.

'If I lived in Skavanga, I'd come here to recharge my batteries.'

Which was exactly what she did. She sometimes came to the cabin just for a change of pace. It helped her to relax and get back in the race.

And it was high time she stopped finding points of contact between them, Britt warned herself, or she'd be convincing herself that fate was giving her a sign. There was no sign. There was no Emir and Britt. It seemed they got on outside sex and business, but that was it.

'What are you thinking?' he said.

She was resting her chin on her knees when she realised Emir was staring at her.

'Why don't you take your underwear off?' he suggested. 'You can't be comfortable in those soggy scraps.'

'They'll soon dry out,' she said, keeping her head down.

Out of the corner of her eye she saw him shrug, but his expression called her a coward. And he was right. She was usually naked before she reached the door of the sauna—and she'd had sex with this man. Plus, she was hardly a vestal virgin in the first place. But somehow with Emir she felt exposed in all sorts of ways, and her underwear was one small, tiny, infinitesimal piece of armour—and she was hanging onto it. 'I'm going outside,' she announced.

'Excellent. I'm ready for my ice rub, Ms Skavanga.'

'Okay, tough guy, bring a towel. And don't blame me if this is too hard core for you.' Her grand flounce off was ruined by the sight of Emir's grin.

She had used to swim through the snow when she was a little girl—or pretend to—and so she plunged straight in. It wasn't something you stopped to think about. The shock was indescribable. But there was plea-sure too as all her nerve endings shrieked at once. The soft bed of snow was cold but not life threatening. It was invigorating, and wiped her mind clean of any con-cerns she had—

But where was Emir?

She suddenly realised he wasn't with her. Springing up, she looked around. Nothing—just silence and snow. She called his name. Still nothing.

Had he gone back to the hut?

She ran to the window and peered in. It was empty.

The lake—

Dread made her unsteady on her feet as she stumbled towards the water, but then she gusted with relief…and fury as his head appeared above the surface. 'You're mad,' she yelled. 'You never go swimming in the lake on your own. What if something had happened to you?'

'You stole my line,' he said, springing out. 'I'm flat-tered you'd care.'

'Of course I'd care,' she yelled, leaning forward hands on hips. 'What the hell would I tell your people if I lost you in a frozen lake? Don't you dare laugh at me,' she warned when Emir pressed his lips together. 'Don't you—'

'What?' he said sharply. Catching hold of her arms, he dragged her close, but she saw from his eyes that he was only teasing her. 'Didn't I tell you I wanted more?' he growled.

His brows rose, his mouth curved. She could have stamped on his foot—much good it would do her in bare feet. They stared at each other for a long moment, until finally she wrestled herself free. 'You're impos-sible! You're irresponsible and you're a pig-headed pain in the neck.'

'Anything else?'

'You deserve to freeze to death!'

'Harsh,' he commented.

Wrapping both towels around her, she stormed off.

'You're a liability!' she flashed over her shoulder, unable to stare at the gleaming lake water streaming off his naked body a moment longer.

'Come back here. You haven't fulfilled your part of the bargain.'

She stopped at the door to the sauna. Emir's voice was pitched low and sent shivers down her spine. This was another of those 'what am I doing here?' moments…

And as soon as she turned she knew. There was nowhere else on earth she'd rather be. 'My part of the bargain?' she queried.

'Ice,' he said, holding her gaze in a way that shot arousal through her.

'I can't believe you haven't had enough yet.'

'I haven't had nearly enough.'

Those black eyes—that stare—that wicked, sexy mouth—

'You asked for this,' she said, scooping up a couple of handfuls.

She was right about ice melting on Emir. Even now, fresh from the lake, he was red hot, and as the ice scraped across his smooth, bronzed skin it disappeared beneath the warmth of her hands, leaving her with no alternative but to explore the heat of his body.

'That's enough,' she said, stepping back the instant her breathing became ragged. She had been wrong to think she could do this—that she could play with this man—toy with him—amuse herself at his expense. Emir was more than a match for her, and the strength she'd felt beneath her hands had only confirmed her thoughts that his body was hard, while hers was all too soft and yielding.

She didn't need to see his face to know he was smiling again as she went back to the sauna hut. Her hands were trembling as she let herself in, and hot guilt rushed through her as she curled up on the bench with her knees tucked under her chin and her arms wrapped tightly round them. By the time Emir walked in, she had put safety back at the top of her agenda. 'Let me know if you plan any more solo trips in the lake. Forget the sheikh—I don't even have a contact number for your next of kin.'

'Your concern overwhelms me,' Emir said dryly as he poured another ladle of water onto the hot stones.

'Where are you going now?' she said as he turned for the door.

'To choose which birch switch I would like to use,' he said as if she should have known. 'Would you care to join me?'

Talk about a conversation stopper.

CHAPTER SIX

SHE WAS TWISTED into a ferment of lust. Her heart was beating like a drum as she watched Emir selecting a birch twig switch. She loved that his process of elimination was so exacting. She loved that he examined each bunch before trying them out on his muscular calves. Each arc through the air…each short, sharp slap against his skin…made her breath catch. Her head was reeling with all sorts of erotic impressions, though she couldn't help wondering if he ever felt the cold. She had grabbed a robe and fur boots before exiting the hut and was well wrapped up.

He started thrashing his shoulders. This was like an advanced lesson in how to watch, feel and suffer— from the most intense frustration she had ever known.

'What do you think?' His dark eyes were full of humour.

'I think I'll leave you to it,' she said, shaking her head as if to indulge the tourist in him.

'Why so prudish, suddenly?' Emir challenged as she turned to go.

Yes. Why was she so strait-laced with Emir when thrashing the body with birch twigs was a normal part of the traditional sauna routine in Skavanga?

'Don't you want to try it?' Emir called after her with amusement in his voice.

She stopped, realising that however high she raised the bar he jumped over it and raised it yet more for her.

Where would this end?

'I can do it any time,' she said casually. He didn't need to know she was shivering with arousal rather than cold as she headed for the door. She swung it open and the enticing warmth with the mellow scent of hot wood washed over her.

'It's not like you to run away from a challenge, Britt.'

She hadn't closed the door yet. 'You don't know anything about me.'

'Are we going to debate this while our body temperatures drop like a stone?'

His maybe. 'You could always join me in the sauna…' she suggested.

'Or you could join me with the birch twigs.' As Emir laughed she made her decision.

'In your dreams. And you might want to put some clothes on,' she added, heading for the sauna hut.

Slamming the door behind her, she leaned back against it, exhaling shakily. Damn the man! Did nothing faze him? She had dreamed of meeting her match, but now she'd met him she wasn't so sure it was such a good idea. They were too similar—too stubborn—too set on duty—too competitive—too everything.

It was too exhausting!

Flopping down on the bench, she closed her eyes, but that didn't help to blank out the fact that a connection of some sort, that wasn't sex, was growing between them. Crashing into the hut in a blast of energy and frigid air, Emir exclaimed, 'Make room for me,' before she could progress this thought.

'Close the door!'

'Wuss,' he murmured in a way that made her picture his sexy mouth curved in that half-smile.

'I don't like the cold,' she muttered, hugging her knees and burying her face so she didn't have to look at him.

'You could have fooled me! But I guess you'd love the desert,' he said.

She went very still and then forced herself to reach for the ladle so she didn't seem too impressed by this last comment.

'You can't still be cold?' Emir commented as she ladled water onto the hot stones. 'That's enough!'

The small hut was full of steam. She had been ladling the water on autopilot, trying not to think about the possibility of travelling to the desert with Emir, and in doing so was threatening to steam them alive. 'Sorry.' She lifted her shoulders in a careless shrug. 'I got carried away.'

'You certainly did,' Emir agreed as he towelled down.

'It's a long time since I've done the whole sauna ritual thing. I'd forgotten—'

'What fun it was?' Emir interrupted.

'How cold you get,' she argued, picking up the ladle again.

He laughed and took it from her. 'That's enough,' he said as their hands brushed. 'Sit down.' He towered over her, blocking out the light. 'If you want to raise the temperature, just ask me.'

'Very funny.' She glanced up.

Emir shrugged and smiled faintly, making her glad she was wearing a towel. He had no inhibitions, and, in fairness, most people went naked in the sauna, but that only worked if they had no sexual interest in each other.

'How about I build a fire in the fire pit outside?' Emir suggested. 'You don't want to be cooped up in here much longer.'

She had always enjoyed sitting round a blazing fire surrounded by snow and ice, and it would be one heck of a lot safer than this intimate space. 'That's a great idea.'

'I'll call you when I'm ready.'

You do that, she thought, banking Emir's sexy smile.

Her heart thumped on cue when he rapped on the door. Sliding off the bench, she went outside to join him. Emir had built an amazing fire...roaring hot and set to last.

'Nights in the desert can be freezing,' he explained. 'And in some parts a fire is essential to keep mountain lions away. We have amazing wildlife,' he added as she sat down and stretched her feet out. 'Kareshi is a country of great contrasts. We have big modern cities as well as a wilderness where tribal traditions haven't changed in centuries.'

Why was he telling her this? Was he serious about her visiting Kareshi? They were staring at each other again, Britt realised, turning away to pretend interest in the fire. There was no point in getting any closer to Emir when their relationship, such as it was, wasn't going anywhere. Lifting his chin, he stared at her as if he were expecting her to say something. Who knew that Britt Skavanga, lately hotshot businesswoman, as her sisters liked to teasingly call her, could feel so awkward, even shy?

Maybe you should get out of the office more often.

Maybe she should, Britt thought wryly, lacking the

energy for once to argue with her contrary inner voice. Emir had gone quite still, she noticed.

'Do you see them?' he said, looking past her into the trees.

'The deer? Yes,' she murmured. A doe and a fawn were watching them from the safety of the undergrowth. 'They're so beautiful,' she whispered, hardly daring to breathe. 'I always feel close to nature here,' she confided in another whisper.

'As I do in the desert,' Emir murmured back.

There was that connection thing again. It was there whether she liked it or not. And now she stiffened, remembering the warning her mother had given her when Britt was a child. Now she understood why her mother had said the things she had, but as a little girl she had thought her father loud rather than violent, and playful, rather than bullying. Now she knew he'd been a drunk who had prompted her mother to warn all her daughters that men kept you down. Her girls were going to be warriors who went out into the world and made their own way. Britt had grown up with the determination that no man would ever rule her engraved on her heart. And Emir was a forceful man…

His touch on her arm made her flinch, but then she realised he was pointing to the deer watching them. The animals were considering flight, and she wondered if it was Emir's inner stillness holding them. Their brown eyes were wide in gentle faces, and though Emir had moved closer to her he kept space between them, which made her feel relaxed. He had that sort of calming aura—which didn't mean she wasn't intensely aware of him. It was a special moment as they watched the deer watching them. It was as if humans and animals had come together briefly.

'What an amazing encounter,' she breathed as the deer turned and picked their way unhurriedly back through the maze of trees into the depth of the forest.

'Now I'm certain you'd love the desert,' Emir said, turning to smile at her. 'Many think it's just a barren space—'

'But we know better?'

He huffed a laugh, holding her gaze in a way that said he was glad she had understood.

'Maybe one day I'll make it to the desert,' she said, trying not to care too much.

'I'll make sure of it,' Emir said quietly. 'If this deal goes through I'll make sure you visit Kareshi.'

'I'd love to,' she exclaimed impulsively.

How much longer are you going to wear your heart on your sleeve? Britt wondered as Emir flashed her an amused glance and raised a brow. But she could see that a whole world of possibility was opening up, both for her and for Skavanga, and she couldn't pretend that the thought of visiting an emerging country where the vigorous young ruler had already done so much for his people didn't excited her.

'I want you to see what the money from the diamonds can accomplish,' Emir remarked.

Yes, there were benefits for both their countries. 'I will,' she said, more in hope than expectation. 'I think you miss Kareshi,' she added in an attempt to shift the spotlight onto him.

'I love my country. I love my people. I love my life in Kareshi. I love my horses—they're a real passion for me. I breed pure Arabs, though sometimes I strengthen the line of my breeding stock with Criolla ponies from the Argentine pampas.'

'You play polo?'

'Of course, and many polo players are my friends. You will have heard of the Acosta brothers, I'm sure.'

She had heard of the Acosta brothers. Who hadn't? 'I learned to ride at the local stable,' she admitted. 'Just old nags compared to the type of horses you're talking about, but I loved it all the same. I love the sense of freedom, and still ride whenever I get the chance.'

'Something we have in common,' he said.

Something else, she thought, inhaling steadily. Friendships were founded on sharing a passion for life, and there was no doubt that they were opening up to each other. So much for her mother's warning. And, yes, it was dangerous to reveal too much of yourself, but if you didn't, how could you ever get close to anyone?

She had to face facts. Once he had collected the information he needed, Emir would go home—and inviting her to Kareshi was probably just talk. Making her excuses, she stood up to go. Emir stood too.

'No birching?' he asked wryly.

She gave him a crooked smile. 'I'm warm enough, thanks to you.'

'That's right,' he called after her as she walked away. 'You probably deserve a good birching—probably even want it. But you're not getting it from me—'

Britt shook her head in wry acceptance, but Emir didn't turn around as she huffed a laugh. He didn't need to. There was a new sort of ease between them—an understanding, almost.

He caught her at the door of the hut, and, lifting a switch from the rack, he shot her a teasing look. 'Are you quite sure?'

'Certain,' she said, but there was laughter in both their eyes.

Laughter that died very quickly when Emir ran the

switch of twigs very lightly down between her breasts and over her belly to the apex of her thighs. She was instantly aroused and couldn't move, even had she wanted to. She remained motionless as he increased the pressure just enough, moving the bunched twigs with exactly the right degree of delicacy. Her breath came out in a noisy shudder, and all this time Emir was holding her gaze. His eyes told her that he knew exactly what she wanted him to do. Her breathing stalled when he used the switch to ease her legs apart.

'Why deny yourself, Britt?'

'Because I need to get inside where it's warm,' she said lightly, pulling herself together.

Physically, she yearned for everything Emir could give her, Britt realised as she quickly shed her underwear, while emotionally she was a wreck. She felt such a strong connection to him, and knew she would never be able to ignore those feelings—

Better she end this now.

He joined her in the hut. That was a foregone conclusion. The stag didn't abandon the doe when it was cornered. The stag knew what the doe wanted and tracking it was part of the game. They sat opposite each other with the hot stones sizzling between them, and, leaning back, Emir gave her a look—just a slight curve at the corner of his sexy mouth.

'What?' she said, knowing he could hardly have avoided noticing that she was naked.

'Now we get really hot,' he said.

CHAPTER SEVEN

As Emir's familiar warmth and scent flared in her senses and his arms gathered her in, Britt felt a new energy flooding through her. She even spared a foolish moment to wish it could always be like this—that he was really hers, and that these strong arms and this strong body would sometimes take over so she could take time out occasionally. But that was so ridiculous she had no difficulty blanking it out. She took one last look at a world where desire for a man could grow into friendship, and where that friendship could grow into love. That was just childhood fantasy. She'd settle for lust.

Holding her face between his hands, Emir made her look at him. Gazing into the burning stare of a man who knew so much about her body made it easy to forget her doubts. Her face must have shown this transition, because he brushed her lips with his. And from there it was an easy slide into a passionate embrace that ended with Emir manoeuvring her into a comfortable position on the bench—which just happened to be under him.

'Is there any part of this you don't like?' he said, smiling down at her.

She liked everything—too much—and at what risk to her heart? Right now she didn't care as another part of Britt Skavanga, warrior woman, chipped off and floated away. At one time sex was little more than a normal function for her, like eating or sleeping, but now…

Now that wasn't nearly enough.

But Emir's hands were distracting her, and as he traced the line of her spine she embraced the feelings inside her. They were so strong she could hardly ignore them. She wanted this man. She wanted him so badly. She wanted to be one with him in every way. Unfortunately, Emir's approach to sex was much like hers had used to be, and being on the receiving end of that was very different from doling it out. But then her mind filled with pleasure as his lips caressed her neck. He knew just how to work her hot spots until she softened against him and relaxed. She had always taken the lead in the past—she had been the one who knew what she was doing and where she was going, the one who was completely in control—but with Emir there was no control. She was his.

'I love your body,' he said as she writhed beneath him.

'I love yours too.' How could she not?

Emir was built on a heroic scale. She doubted she had ever met a bigger man. There wasn't a spare inch of unnecessary flesh on his hard, toned body, and each muscle was clearly delineated after his strenuous physical exercise in the lake. He was every bit the soldier, the fighter, the leader, yet he had the most sensitive hands. She groaned as he massaged her scalp with his fingertips.

'What do you want, Britt?' he murmured.

'Do you really need me to answer that?'

'I like you to tell me,' he said.

Emir's voice had the power to arouse her almost as

much as the man himself. Raising her chin, she took a deep breath and then told him what she wanted.

'So open your legs wider,' he said.

Her first thought was, No. I can't do that—not while you're looking down at me.

'Wider,' he said.

She wanted this. He excited her—

'Wider still…'

'I can't—you're merciless—'

'Yes, I am,' he agreed in the same soft tone.

'Enough,' she begged him, reaching out. She needed human contact. She needed closeness more than anything. She needed a kiss—a tender kiss. She still longed for the illusion that they were close in every way, Britt realised, feeling a pang of regret for what could never be.

He had never seen anything more beautiful than Britt at this moment, when every part of her was glowing and aroused. His desire to be joined to her was overwhelming, but something as special as this could not be rushed. It must be appreciated and savoured. One of the so-called erotic secrets of Kareshi was nothing more than this lingering over pleasure. Making time for pleasure was a so much a national pursuit he had been forced to persuade the Kareshi people to balance their country's business needs against it, but he would never wish these old traditions to die out. In fact, he had every intention of fostering them, and as Britt reached for him he took her wrists in a firm grip. 'Not yet,' he whispered.

'Don't you want me?' she said, arching her back as she displayed her breasts to best advantage.

She had no idea how much.

He held her locked in his stare as she sat up. He even

allowed her to lace her fingers through his hair, binding him to her. Britt was easy to read. She was already on the edge. Intuition had always helped him in the past— in all sorts of situations, and now this. With Britt he mastered his own desires by channelling his thoughts into all the things that intrigued him about her.

'How can you bear to wait?' she complained.

'I bear it because I know what's best for you,' he said. 'I know what you need and I know the best way to give it to you.'

'How do you know?' she said, writhing with impatience.

On the sexual front that was all too obvious, but knowing Britt wasn't so hard. She was the oldest child, always trying to do her best, the lab-rat for her sisters, the one who would have been given the strictest upbringing by her parents. Britt was used to bearing the weight of responsibility on her shoulders, and with duties at home and then duties in the business she hadn't had much time to explore life, let alone discover the nuances of sex and how very good it could be.

'So, how did you like our Nordic traditions?' she murmured against his mouth.

Distracted, he brushed a kiss against her lips. 'I like them a lot. I'd like to know more. I'd like to know more about you—'

The look of surprise on her face almost broke the erotic spell for him, and then she said with touching honesty, 'I'd like to know more about you and your country.'

'Maybe you will.'

Closing his eyes, he inhaled her wildflower scent, and realised then that the thought of never smelling it again was unthinkable. He was still on guard, of course.

There was still a business deal to do and it would be unwise to underestimate Britt Skavanga. She was everything he had been warned to expect…and so much more.

When Emir kissed her she was glad of his arms supporting her, because he didn't just kiss her breath away, he kissed her thoughts away too. It felt so good to drop her guard and lose herself in sensation, shut out the business robot she had become. It was good to feel sensation spreading in tiny rivers of fire through her veins, and even better to feel Emir's erection resting heavily against her thigh, because that said he wanted her as much as she wanted him. She groaned with anticipation when he nudged her thighs apart. Moving between them, he started teasing her with delicate touches until she thought she would go mad for him.

'Wrap your legs around me,' he instructed, staring deep into her eyes.

'Don't make me wait,' she warned, but in a way she was glad when he soothed her with kisses and caresses first. She cried out and urged him on. There were no certainties other than the fact that she was being drawn deeper into a dangerous liaison with him.

As if sensing her unease, he took her face in his big, warm hands and drugged her with kisses. Gentle to begin with, they grew deeper and firmer as the embers inside her sparked and flared. She loved it when he took possession of her mouth, and loved it even more when he took possession of her body. She loved being held so firmly. She loved the powerful emotions inside her.

'Have you changed your mind?' he said as she tried to rein them in.

She denied this, and then he did something so amazing she couldn't have stopped him if she had tried. A shaking cry escaped her throat as he sank slowly deep inside her. She could never be fully prepared for Emir. The sheer size of him stole the breath from her lungs. He was such an intuitive lover. He understood every part of her and how she responded. He knew her limits and never stepped over them, while his hands and mouth worked magic. Today he was using the seductive language of Kareshi—soft and guttural, husky and persuasive—to both encourage and excite her. It must have succeeded because she found herself pressing her legs wide for him with the heel of her palms against her thighs.

'Good,' he approved, thrusting even deeper.

She cried out his name repeatedly as he moved rhythmically and reliably towards the inevitable conclusion. But suddenly some madness overcame them, and control was no longer possible as they fought their way to release.

She was still shuddering with aftershocks minutes later. Her internal muscles closed around him gratefully, to an indescribably delicious beat.

Neither of them spoke for quite a while. They had both experienced the same thing—something out of the ordinary, she thought as Emir stared down at her. At last his eyes were full of everything she had longed to see.

'I take it you enjoyed that?' he murmured, and, withdrawing gently, he helped her to sit up.

'And you?' she said, resting her cheek against his chest.

'I have one suggestion—'

She glanced up.

'Next time we try a bed.'

His grin infected her. 'Now there's a novel thought,'

she agreed, but after she had rested on him for a moment or two harsh reality intruded and she remembered who she was, who he was, and the parts they played in this drama.

Lifting her chin, she put on the old confident face. 'Don't get ahead of yourself, mister. I sleep alone.'

'Who mentioned sleeping?' Emir argued.

'Do you always have to show such perfect good sense?'

'With you, I think I do,' he said, smiling, unrepentant.

Emir was probably the one man she was prepared to take instruction from, Britt concluded as she showered down later in her en-suite bathroom at the cabin, if only because the pay-off was so great. And she wasn't just thinking about the sexual pay-off, but the pay-off that was making her sing and waltz around the bathroom like a fruit-loop—the pay-off that made her feel all warm and fuzzy inside—and optimistic about the future—about everything. She felt suddenly as if anything could happen—as if the boundaries of Skavanga and her job had fallen away, leaving a world full of possibility. And the desert kingdom of Kareshi was definitely the stand out country in that world waiting to be discovered.

Of course, she must visit Emir's homeland as he had suggested. If the deal went through it would be wrong to accept the consortium's investment without wanting to know as much as she possibly could about the benefits the diamonds would bring to both countries. Perhaps there could be reciprocal cultural and educational opportunities—anything was possible. She longed to get stuck into it—to get out of the office and meet people at last. Her mind was blazing with ideas. No dream seemed too far-fetched.

Showering down after his unique encounter with Britt, Sharif's thoughts were arranged in several compartments. The first was all to do with Britt the businesswoman. She was meticulous and had held the company together when many would have failed. Her attention to detail was second to none—as he had learned when it had taken him several hours, rather than the usual five minutes, to pore over her first agenda and find a hole. She was clear-headed and quick-thinking in her business life—

And an emotional mess when it came to anything else.

Her life was tied up in duty, but she wanted it all. He guessed she heard the clock ticking, but she didn't know how to escape from her work long enough to find the fulfilment she craved—the satisfaction of raising her own family and extending her sphere of influence in the workplace too. She did everything she could to support her sisters while they studied and campaigned for this and that, but they didn't seem to stop and think that Britt deserved some fulfilment too.

And neither should he, he reminded himself. He had one duty, one goal, and one responsibility, which was to the men who had come in with him on this deal. Business always came first, because business fed improvements in Kareshi, and only then could he afford to pause to wonder if there was anything missing from his life—

Britt?

Any man would be missing a woman like Britt in his life. She was exceptional. She was an intriguing mix of control and abandonment, and it seemed to him that the only time Britt let go was during sex, which made cutting the best deal possible a challenging prospect, but not impossible.

Business, always business, he thought, towelling down. He liked that Britt was part of that business. He had always loved a challenge and Britt was a challenge. Securing the towel around his waist, he picked up his razor to engage in the one battle he usually lost. His beard grew faster than he could shave it off, but at least the ritual soothed him and gave him time to think.

Shaking his head as if that could shake thoughts of Britt out of it, he rinsed his face and raked his thick, unruly hair into some semblance of order. The deal was a tantalising prospect and he would bring it in. Between them he and his friends had the means and the skill and the outlets necessary to transform dull, uncut diamonds into sparkling gems that would shimmer with fire as they shivered against a woman's skin. Britt believed she held all the cards, and could cut the better deal, but he held the joker.

Stepping into jeans, he tugged on a plain back top, and fastened his belt before reaching for the phone. Some decisions were harder to take than others, and this was harder than most. Britt had all the instincts of a man inside the body of a woman, but she had a woman's emotions, which held her back when it came to clear thinking in a deal like this where family was involved. He wished he could protect her from the fall-out from this call, but his duty was clear. This wasn't for him alone, but for the consortium, and for Kareshi. In the absence of her brother, Britt led her tribe as he did, making her a worthy adversary. He just had to hope she could handle this new twist in the plot as compe-

tently as she had coped with other obstacles life had
thrown at her.

He drummed his fingers impatiently as he waited
for the call to connect. Three rings later the call was
answered. He hesitated, which was definitely a first
for him, but the die had been cast on the day he had sat
down to research the share structure of Skavanga Mining and had discovered that the major shareholder was
not in fact the three sisters, but their missing brother,
Tyr Skavanga. More complicated still was that, for reasons of his own, Tyr didn't want his sisters to know
where he was. Having given his word, Emir would have
to keep that from Britt even though Tyr's long-distance
involvement in the deal would swing the balance firmly
in the consortium's favour.

'Hello, Tyr,' he said, settling down into what he knew
would be a long call.

CHAPTER EIGHT

HE WAS PACKING? *Emir was packing?* She had come downstairs after her shower expecting to find him basking in front of a roaring fire—which he would have banked up, perhaps with a drink in hand and one waiting for her on the table. She had anticipated more getting-to-know-you time. That was what couples did when they'd grown closer after sex…

And they had grown closer, Britt reassured herself, feeling painfully obvious in banged-up jeans, simple top and bare feet. She felt as if, in this relaxed state, all her feelings were on display. And all those feelings spoke of closeness and intimacy with Emir. She had dressed in anticipation of continuing ease between them. She had dressed as she would dress when her sisters were around. And now she felt vulnerable and exposed. And utterly ridiculous for having let her guard down so badly.

How could she have got this so wrong?

She watched him from the doorway of his bedroom as Emir folded his clothes, arranging them in a bag that he could sling casually over his shoulder. He must have known she was standing there, but he didn't say a word. The chill seemed to creep up from the floor and consume her. Even her face felt cold.

What had gone wrong?

What was wrong was that Emir didn't care and she had refused to see that. He had come here to do a job and his job was done. He had taken samples for analysis and had seen the mine for himself. He had weighed her up and interviewed her colleagues. His only job now was to pack up and leave. What had she been? An unexpected bonus on the side? She had no part to play in Emir's plans, he'd made that clear. Why had she ever allowed herself to believe that she had? All that talk of Kareshi and the desert was just that—talk.

Her throat felt tight. Her mouth was dry. She felt numb. Anything she said in this situation would sound ridiculous. And what was the point of having a row when she had no call on this man? She had enjoyed him as much as he had enjoyed her. Was it his fault if she couldn't move on?

All this was sound reasoning, but reason didn't allow for passion, for emotion—for any of the things she felt for Emir. And out of bitter disappointment at his manner towards her—or rather his lack of…anything, really—came anger. What had he meant by staring into her eyes and suggesting they should take sex to the bedroom next time? Was that concern for her? Or was Emir more concerned about getting grazes on his knees? She had laughed with and trusted this man. Everything had changed for her, because she'd thought… Because she'd thought…

She didn't have a clue what she'd thought, Britt realised. She only knew she had given herself completely to a man, something she'd never done before, and now, just as her mother had predicted, she was paying the price. But she would not play the role of misused mistress and give him the chance to mock.

'You're leaving?' she said coolly. 'Already?'

'My job here's done,' Emir confirmed, straightening up. He turned to face her. 'My flight plan is filed. I leave right away.'

When did he file his flight plan? Immediately after making love to her?

'Do you have transport to the airport?' She wasn't so petty she would let him call a cab. She would take him to the airport if she had to.

'My people are coming for me,' he said, turning back to zip up his bag.

Of course. 'Oh, good,' she said, going hot and cold in turn as she chalked up the completeness of his plan as just one more insult to add to the rest. He'd had sex with her first and then had called his people to come and get him. He'd used her—

As she had used men in the past.

Her heart lurched as their eyes met. Mistake. Now he could see how badly she didn't want him to go.

'I have to report back to the consortium, Britt,' he said, confirming this assumption.

'Of course.' She cleared her throat and arranged her features in a composed mask. She had never been at such a disadvantage where a man was concerned. But that was because she had never known anyone like Emir before and had always prided herself on being able to read people. She had not read him. They were like two strangers, out of sync, out of context, out of time.

She stood in embarrassed silence. With no small talk to delay him, let alone some siren song with which to change his mind, she could only wait for him to leave.

'Thank you for your hospitality, Britt,' he said, shouldering the bag.

Her hospitality? Did that include the sex? Her face

was composed, but as Emir moved to shake her hand she stood back.

Emir didn't react one way or the other to this snub. 'I'll wait for test results on the samples, and if all goes well you will hear from my lawyers in the next few weeks.'

'Your lawyers?' Her head was reeling by now, with business and personal thoughts hopelessly mixed.

'Forgive me, Britt.' Emir paused with his hand on the door. 'I meant, of course, the lawyers acting for the consortium will be in touch with you.'

Suddenly all the anger and hurt inside her exploded into fury, which manifested itself in an icy question. 'And what if I get a better offer in the meantime?'

'Then you must consider it and we will meet again. I should tell you that the consortium has been in touch with your sisters, and they have already agreed—'

'You've spoken to Eva and Leila?' she cut in. He'd done that without speaking to her? She couldn't take any more in than she already had—and she certainly couldn't believe that her sisters would do a deal without speaking to her first.

'My people have spoken to your sisters,' Emir explained.

'And you didn't think to tell me?' *They didn't think to tell me?* She was flooded with hurt and pain.

'I just have.' A muscle flicked in his jaw.

'So all the time we've been here—' Outrage boiled in her eyes. 'I think you'd better go,' she managed tensely. Suddenly, all that mattered was speaking to her sisters so she could find out what the hell was going on.

Meanwhile, Emir was checking round the room, just to be sure he hadn't forgotten anything, presumably. He didn't care a jot about her, she realised with a cold rush of certainty. This had only ever been about the deal. How convenient to keep her distracted here while the consortium's lackeys acted behind her back. How very clever of Emir. And how irredeemably stupid of her.

'If you've left anything I'll send it on,' she said coldly, just wanting him to go.

How could her heart still betray her when Emir's brooding stare switched to her face?

'I knew I could count on you,' he said as her stupid heart performed the customary leap.

Emir's impassive stare turned her own eyes glacial. 'Well, you've got what you wanted from me, so you might as well go. You'll get nothing else here.'

The inky brows rose, but Emir remained silent. She just hoped her barb had stabbed home. But no.

'This is business, Britt, and there is no emotion in business. I wish I could tell you more, but—'

'Please—spare me.' She drew herself up. 'Goodbye, Emir.'

She didn't follow him out. She wouldn't give him the satisfaction. She listened to him jog down the stairs, while registering the tenderness of a body that had been very well used, and heard him stride across the main room downstairs where they had been so briefly close. It was as if Emir were stripping the joy out of the cabin she loved with every step he took, and each of those departing steps served as a reminder that she had wasted her feelings on someone who cared for nothing in this world apart from business.

Apart from her sisters and Tyr, that had been how she was not so very long ago, Britt conceded as the front door closed behind Emir.

She hadn't even realised she had stopped breathing

until she heard a car door slam and she drew in a desperate, shuddering breath.

There were times when he would gladly exchange places with the grooms who worked in his stables and this was one of them, but harsh decisions had to be made. He thought he could feel Britt's anguished stare on his back as he held up his hand to hail the black Jeep that had come to collect him. His men would take him back to the airport and his private jet. His mind was still full of her when he climbed into the passenger seat and they drove him away. It was better to leave now before things became really complicated.

Her sense of betrayal by Emir—and, yes, even more so by her sisters—was indescribable. And for once both Eva and Leila were out of touch by phone. She had tried them constantly since Emir had left, prowling around the cabin like a wounded animal, unable to settle or do anything until she had spoken to them. Even her beloved cabin had let her down. It failed to soothe her this time. She should never have brought Emir here. He had tainted her precious memories.

Not wanting to face the fact that she had been less than focused, she turned on every light in the cabin, but it still felt empty. There was no reply from her sisters, so all she could do was dwell on what she'd seen through the window when he'd left—Emir climbing into a Jeep and being driven away. She'd got the sense of other big men in the vehicle, shadowy, and no doubt armed. Where there were such vast resources up for grabs, no one took any chances. She had been kidding herself if she had thought that bringing investors in would be easy to handle. She was up against a powerful and well-oiled machine. She should have known when each man in the consortium was a power in his own right, and she was on her own—

So? Get used to it! There was no time for self-pity. This was all about protecting her sisters, whatever they'd done. They weren't to blame. They had no idea what it took to survive in the cut-throat world of business—she didn't want them to know. She would protect them as she always had.

She nearly jumped out of her skin when the phone rang, and she rushed to pick it up. Mixed feelings when she did so, because it was Eva, her middle and least flexible sister, calling. 'Eva—'

'You rang?' Eva intoned. 'Seven missed calls, Britt? What's going on?'

Where to begin? Suddenly, Britt was at a loss, but then her mind cleared and became as unemotional as it usually was where business was concerned. 'The man from the consortium just left the cabin. He said you and Leila signed something?' Britt waited tensely for her sister to respond, guessing Eva would be doing ten things at once. 'So, what have you signed?' Britt pressed, controlling her impatience.

'All we did was give permission for the consortium's people to enter the offices to start their preliminary investigations.'

'Why didn't you speak to me first?'

'Because we couldn't get hold of you.'

And now she could only rue the day she had left Skavanga to show Emir the mine.

'We thought we were helping you move things on.'

Britt could accept that. The sooner the consortium's accountants had completed their investigations, the sooner she could bring some investment into Skavanga

Mining and save the company. 'So you haven't agreed to sell your shares?'

'Of course not. What do you take me for?'

'I don't want to argue with you, Eva. I'm just worried—'

'You know I don't know the first thing about the business,' Eva countered. 'And I'm sorry you got landed with it when our parents died. I do know there are a thousand things you'd rather do.'

'Never mind that now—I need to help people at home. I'm coming back—'

'Before you go, how did you get on with him?"

'Who?' Britt said defensively.

'You know—the man who was at the mine with you—the sheikh's man.'

'Oh, you mean Emir.'

'What?'

'Emir,' Britt repeated.

'Well, that's original,' Eva murmured with a smile in her voice. 'Did the Black Sheikh come up with any more titles to fool you, or just the one?'

Britt started to say something and then stopped. 'Sorry?'

'Oh, come on,' Eva exclaimed impatiently. 'I guess he was quite a man, but I can't believe your brain has taken up permanent residence below your belt. You know your thesaurus as well as anyone: emir, potentate, person of rank. Have I rung any bells yet?'

'But he said his name was—' Hot waves of shame washed over her. She was every bit as stupid as she had thought herself when Emir left, only more so.

'Since when have you believed everything you're told, Britt?' Eva demanded.

Since she met a man who told her that his name was Emir.

She had to speak to him. She would speak to him, Britt determined icily, just as soon as she had finished this call to her sister.

'You haven't fallen for him, have you?' Eva said shrewdly.

'No, of course not,' Britt fired back.

There was a silence that suggested Eva wasn't entirely convinced. Too bad. Whatever Britt might have felt for Emir was gone now. Gone completely. Finished. Over. Dead. Gone.

'You should have taken him for a roll in the snow so you could both cool down.'

'I did,' she admitted flatly. 'He loved it.'

'Sounds like my kind of guy—'

'This isn't funny, Eva.'

'No,' Eva agreed, turning serious. 'You've made a fool of yourself and you don't like it. Turns out you're not the hotshot man-eater you thought you were.'

'But I'm still a businesswoman,' Britt murmured thoughtfully, 'and you know what they say.'

'I'm sure you're going to tell me,' Eva observed dryly.

'Don't get mad, get even.'

'That's what I was afraid of,' Eva commented under her breath. 'Just don't cut off your nose to spite your face. Don't screw this deal after putting so much effort into it.'

'Don't worry, I won't.'

'So what are you going to do?' Eva pressed, concern ringing in her voice.

For betraying her—for allowing his people to approach her sisters while Britt and he were otherwise engaged?

'I'm going to follow him to Kareshi. I'm going to track him down. I'm going to ring his office to try and find out where he is. I'll go into the desert if I have to. I'm going to find the bastard and make him pay.'

CHAPTER NINE

KARESHI...

She was actually here. It hardly seemed possible. For all her bitter, mixed-up thoughts when it came to the man she had called Emir and must now learn to call His Majesty Sheikh Sharif al Kareshi, Britt couldn't help but be dazzled by her first sight of the ocean of sand stretching away to a purple haze following the curve of the earth. She craned her neck, having just caught sight of the glittering capital city. It couldn't stand in greater contrast to the desert.

Just as her thoughts of the man the world called the Black Sheikh couldn't have stood in starker contrast to the universal approval the man enjoyed. How could he fool so many people? How could he fool her?

That last question was easily answered. Her body had done that for her, yearning for a man when it should freeze at the very thought of him—if she had any sense.

As the city came into clearer view and she saw all the amazing buildings she got a better picture of the Black Sheikh's power and his immense wealth. It seemed incredible that she was here, and that His Majesty Sheikh Sharif had been her lover—

That she had been so easily fooled.

'The captain has switched the seat-belt sign on.'

'Oh, yes, thank you,' she said glancing up, glad of the distraction. Any distraction to take her mind off that man was welcome.

Having secured her belt, she continued to stare avidly out of the window. Her life to date hadn't allowed for much time outside Skavanga, and from what she could see from the plane Kareshi couldn't have been more different. The thought of exploring the city and meeting new people was exciting in spite of all the other things she had to face. An ivory beach bordered the city, and beyond that lay a tranquil sea of clear bright blue, but it was the wilderness that drew her attention. The Black Sheikh was down there somewhere. His people had told her this in an attempt to put her off. They didn't know her if they thought she would be dismayed to learn His Majesty was deep in the desert with his people. She would find him and she would confront him. She had every reason to do so, if only to learn the result of the trials on the mineral samples he had taken from the mine. She suspected he would agree to see her. His people were sure to have told him that she had been asking for him and, like Britt, the Black Sheikh flinched from nothing.

Another glance out of the window revealed a seemingly limitless carpet of umber and sienna, gold and tangerine, and over this colourful, if alien landscape the black shadow of the aircraft appeared to be creeping with deceptive stealth. The desert was a magical place and she was impatient to be travelling through it. Would she find Sheikh Sharif? The ice fields of Skavanga were apparently featureless, but that was never completely true, and where landmarks failed there was always GPS. Tracking down the ruler of Kareshi would be a challenge, but not one she couldn't handle.

* * *

Shortly after she reached the hotel Britt received a call from Eva to say that one of their main customers for the minerals they mined had gone down, defaulting on a payment to Skavanga Mining, and leaving the company dangerously exposed. It was the last thing she needed, and her mind was already racing on what to do for the best when Eva explained that the consortium had stepped in.

'I think you need to speak to the sheikh to find out the details.'

'That's my intention,' Britt assured her sister, feeling that the consortium's net was slowly closing over her family business.

As soon as she ended the call she tried once again to speak to a member of the sheikh's staff to arrange an appointment as a matter of urgency. Audience with His Majesty was booked up for months in advance, some snooty official informed her. And, no, His Majesty had *certainly not* left any message for a visitor from a *mining* company. This was said as if mining were some sleazy, disreputable occupation.

So speaks a man who has probably never got his hands dirty in his life, Britt thought, pulling the phone away from her ear. She had been placing calls non-stop from her bedroom for the past two hours—to Sharif's offices, to his palace, to the country's administrative offices, and even to her country's diplomatic representative in the city.

Okay. Calm down, she told herself, taking a deep breath as she paced the room. Let's think this through. There was a number she could call, and this really was a wild card. Remembering Emir telling her about his love of horses, she stabbed in the number for His Majesty's stables.

The voice that answered was young and female and it took Britt a couple of breaths to compute this, as her calls so far had led Britt to believe that only men worked for the sheikh and they all had tent poles up their backsides.

'Hello,' the pleasant female voice said again. 'Jasmina Kareshi speaking…'

The Black Sheikh's sister! Though Princess Jasmina sounded far too relaxed to be a princess. 'Hello. This is Britt Skavanga speaking. I wonder if you could help me?'

'Call me Jazz,' the friendly voice on the other end of the line insisted as Jazz went on to explain that her brother had in fact been in touch some time ago to warn her that Britt was due to arrive in the country.

'How did he find out?' Britt exclaimed with surprise.

'Are you serious?' Jazz demanded.

Jazz's upbeat nature was engaging, and as the ruler of Kareshi's sister proceeded to tell Britt that her brother knew everything that was going on in Kareshi at least ten minutes before it happened Britt got the feeling that in different circumstances Jazz and she might have been friends.

'As he's not here, I'm supposed to be helping you any way I can,' Jazz explained. 'I can only apologise that it's taken so long for the two of us to get in touch, but I've been tied up with my favourite mare at the stables while she was giving birth.'

'Please don't apologise,' Britt said quickly. She was just glad to have someone sensible to talk to. 'I hope everything went well for your horse.'

'Perfectly,' Jazz confirmed, adding in an amused

tone, 'I imagine it went a lot better for me and my mare than it did for you without a formal introduction to my brother's stuffy staff.'

Diplomacy was called for, Britt concluded. 'They did what they could,' she said cagily.

'I bet they did,' Jazz agreed wryly.

This was really dangerous. Not only had she fallen for the Black Sheikh masquerading as Emir, but now she was starting to get on with his sister.

'My brother's in the desert,' Jazz confirmed. 'Let me give you the GPS—'

'Thanks.'

Jazz proceeded to dispense GPS coordinates for a Bedouin camp in the desert as casually as if she were directing Britt to the local mall. Britt was able to draw a couple of possible conclusions from this. Sharif had not wanted his staff to know about the connection between them—possibly because as she was a woman in a recently reformed and previously male-dominated country they wouldn't treat her too well. But at least he had entrusted the news of her arrival to Jazz. She'd give him the benefit of the doubt this one time. Just before signing off, she checked with Jazz that the car hire company she had decided on had the best vehicles for trekking in the desert.

'It should be the best,' Jazz exclaimed. 'Like practically everything else in Kareshi, my brother owns it.'

Of course he did. And he thought Skavanga Mining was in the bag too. Not just an investment, but a takeover. There was no time to lose. Having promised to keep in touch with Jazz, she cut the line.

She had a moment—a fluttering heart, sweaty palms moment—when she knew it would have been far safer to deal with the Black Sheikh from a distance, preferably half a world away in Skavanga. Sharif was too confident for her liking, telling his sister about Britt's arrival in Kareshi as if he knew all her arrangements. According to Jazz it was very likely that he did, Britt reasoned, more eager than ever to get into the desert to confront him. And this time she would definitely confine their talks to business. She might be a slow learner, but she never made the same mistake twice.

He wasn't surprised that Britt had decided to track him down in the desert. He would have been more surprised if she had remained in Skavanga doing nothing. He admired her for not taking anything lying down. Well, almost anything, he mused, a smile hovering around his mouth. He did look forward to taking her on a bed one day.

Stretching out his naked body on the bank of silken cushions in the sleeping area of his tent, he turned his thoughts to business. Business had always been a game to him—a game he never lost, though with Britt it was different. He wanted to include her. He knew about the customer going bankrupt leaving Skavanga Mining in the lurch. He also knew there was nothing Britt could have done about it even had she been in Skavanga, though he doubted she would see it that way. He had been forced to get in touch with Tyr again to fast-track the deal, and with Britt on her way to the desert maybe he would get the chance to put her straight. He didn't like this subterfuge Tyr had forced upon him, though he could understand the reasons for it.

He rose and bathed in the pool formed by an underground stream that bubbled up beside his sleeping quarters. Donning his traditional black robes, he ran impatient hands through his damp black hair. Jasmina had contacted him to say that Britt had landed safely and would soon be joining him. Not soon enough, he thought as one of the elders of the tribe gave a discreet cough from the entrance to the tent to attract his attention.

A tent was a wholly inadequate description for the luxurious pavilion in which this noble tribe had insisted on housing him, Sharif reflected as he strode in lightweight sandals across priceless rugs to greet the old man. A simple bivouac would have been enough for him, but this was a palatial marquee fitted out as if for some mythical potentate. It was in fact a priceless ancient artefact, full of antique treasures, which had been carefully collected and preserved over centuries by the wandering tribesmen who kept these sorts of tents permanently at the ready to welcome their leader.

The elder informed him that the preparations for Britt's arrival were now in place. Sharif thanked him with no hint of his personal thoughts on his face, but it amused him to think that an experienced businesswoman like Britt had shown no compunction in attempting to throw him off stride by introducing him to a variety of Nordic delights. It remained to be seen how she would react when he turned the tables on her. How would she like being housed in the harem, for instance?

The elderly tribesman insisted on showing him round the harem tent set aside for Britt. It was a great deal more luxurious than even Sharif's regal pavilion, though admittedly it was a little short on seating areas. The large, luxuriously appointed space was dominated by an enormous bank of silken cushions carefully arranged into the shape of a bed enclosed by billowing white silk curtains. The harem tent had one purpose and one purpose only—a thought that curved his lips in a smile, if only because Britt would soon realise where she was staying, and would be incensed. Teasing her was one of his favourite pastimes. How long was it going to take her to realise that?

Thanking his elderly guide, he ducked his head and left the tent. Pausing a moment, he soaked in the purposeful bustle of a community whose endless travels along unseen paths through a wilderness that stretched seemingly to infinity never failed to amaze him. He didn't bring many visitors to the desert, believing the change from their soft lives in the city to the rigours of life in an encampment would be too much for them, but Britt was different. She was adventurous and curious, and would relish every moment of a challenge like this.

Spending time with his people was always a pleasure for him. It gave him a welcome break from the constant baying of the media—to see his face, to know his life, to know him. And, more importantly, it gave him the chance to live alongside his people and understand their needs. On this visit the elders had asked for more travelling schools, as well as more mobile clinics and hospitals. They would have them. He would make sure of it.

No wonder he was passionate about the diamond deal, Sharif reflected as some of the children ran up to him, clustering around a man who, in their eyes, was merely a newcomer in the camp. He hunkered down so they were all on eye level, while the children examined his prayer beads and the heavily decorated scabbard of his *khanjar*, the traditional Kareshi dagger that he wore at his side.

This was his joy, he realised as he watched the children's dark, inquisitive eyes, and their busy little hands as they examined these treasures. They were the future of his country, and he would allow nothing to put a dent in the prospects of these children. He had banished his unscrupulous relatives with the express purpose of allowing Kareshi to grow and flourish, and he would support his people with whatever it took.

He was still the warrior Sheikh, Sharif reflected as the children were called away for supper. His people expected it of their leader, and it was a right that he had fought for, and that was in his blood. But he did have a softer side that he didn't show the world, and that side of him longed for a family, and for closeness and love. He hadn't known that as a child. He hadn't even realised that he'd missed it until he spent more time here in the desert with his people. What he wouldn't give to know the closeness they shared...

He stopped outside the tent they had prepared for Britt, and felt a rush of gratitude for the heritage his people had so carefully preserved. As he fingered the finely woven tassels holding back the curtains over the opening his thoughts strayed back to Britt. They had never really left her.

It wasn't as if she hadn't changed a tyre before—

Famously, she had changed one on the very first day she had met Sharif. But that had been on a familiar vehicle with tools she had used before, and on a hard surface, while this was sand.

As soon as she raised the Jeep on the jack, it slipped and thumped down hard, narrowly missing her feet. Hands on her hips, she considered her options. It was a beautiful night. The sky was clear, the moon was bright, and she had parked in the shadow of a dune where she was sheltered from the wind. It was lovely—if she could just calm down. And, maybe she shouldn't have set out half cock with only the thought of seeing Emir/Sharif

again in her head. But she was where she was, and had
to get on with it.

She had never seen so many stars before, Britt realised, staring up. What a beautiful place this was.
There was no pollution of any kind. A sea of stars and
a crescent moon hung overhead. And there was no need
for panic, she reasoned, turning back to the Jeep. She
had water, fuel, and plenty of food. The GPS was up and
running, and according to that she was only around fifteen miles away from the encampment. The best thing
she could do was wait until the morning when she would
try again to wedge the wheels and stop them slipping.
As a sensible precaution, and because she didn't want
Jazz to worry, she texted Sharif's sister: *Flat tyre. No
prob. I'll sleep 4WD then change it am and head 2
camp.*

A reply came through almost immediately: *I hve yr
coordinates. Do u hve flares? Help o—*

The screen blanked. She tried again. She shook the
phone. She screamed obscenities at it. She banged it on
her hand and screamed again. She tried switching it off
and rebooting it.

It was dead.

So what had Jazz meant by that last message? Help
was on its way? Or help off-road in the middle of the
desert at night was out of the question?

Heaving a breath, she stared up, and blinked to find
the sky completely changed. Half was as beautiful as
the last time she looked, which was just a few seconds
ago, while the other half was sullen black. A prickle of
unease crept down her spine. And then a spear of fright
when she heard something…the rushing sound of a fe-
rocious wind. It was like all her childhood nightmares
come at once. Something monstrous was on its way—

what, she couldn't tell. The only certainty was that it was getting closer all the time.

Her hands were trembling, Britt realised as she buttoned the phone inside the breast pocket of her shirt. Not much fazed her, but now she wished she had a travelling companion who knew the desert. Sharif would know. This was his home territory. Sharif would know what to do.

The elders had invited him to eat with them around the campfire. The respect they showed him was an honour he treasured. Here in the wildest reaches of the desert he might be their leader, but he could always learn from his people and this was a priceless opportunity for him to speak to them about their concerns. They talked on long into the night, and by the time he left them he was glad he could bring them good news about renewed investment and the realisation of their plans. He didn't go straight back to his tent. He felt restless for no good reason other than the fact that the palm trees seemed unnaturally still to him, as if they were waiting for something to happen. He had a keen weather nose and tonight the signs weren't good. He stared up into the clear sky, knowing things could change in a few moments in the desert.

He paced the perimeter of the camp and found himself back at the harem tent where Britt would be housed when she arrived. His mood lightened as he dipped his head to take a look inside. He could just imagine her outraged reaction when she realised where she was staying. He hoped she would at least linger long enough to enjoy some of the delights. The surroundings were so sumptuous it seemed incredible that they could exist outside a maharaja's palace, let alone in the desert. Like his own pavilion, hers had been cleverly positioned around the underground stream. The water was clear and warm and provided a natural bathing pool in a discreetly closed off section of the tent. Solid gold drinking vessels glinted in the mellow light of brass lanterns, while priceless woven rugs felt rich and soft beneath his sandaled feet. The heady scent of incense pervaded everything, but it was the light that was so special. The candles inside the lanterns washed the space with a golden light that gave the impression of a golden room. It certainly wasn't a place to hold a business meeting. This tent was dedicated entirely to pleasure, a fact he doubted Britt would miss. He tried not to smile, but there was everything here a sheikh of old might have required to woo his mistress. The older women of the tribe had heard a female visitor was expected and had approached him with their plan; he couldn't resist.

Would their Leader's friend be pleased to experience some of the very special beauty treatments that had been passed down through generations?

Absolutely, he had replied.

Would she enjoy being dressed in one of the precious vintage robes they had lovingly cleaned and preserved; a robe they carried with them in their treasure chest on their endless travels across the desert?

He didn't even have to think about that one. He was sure she would.

And the food...Would she enjoy their food? Could they make her sweetmeats like the old days; the sort of thing with which the sheikhs of old would tempt their... their...

Their friends? he had supplied helpfully.

'I'm sure she would,' he had confirmed. He had yet to meet a woman who would refuse a decent piece of cake.

His acceptance of all these treats for Britt had put smiles into many eyes, and that was all he cared about.

Their final assurance was that if their sheikh would honour them by entertaining a female visitor in their camp, they would ensure he did so in the old way.

Perfect, he had said, having some idea of what that might entail. He couldn't think of anything his visitor would enjoy more, he had told them.

Imagining Britt's expression when she was treated as a prized concubine was thanks enough, but there was a serious element to this mischief. The older women guided the young, and it was imperative to have them onside so they embraced all the educational opportunities he was opening up to women under his rule. Kareshi would be different—better for all in the future, and on that he was determined.

The peal of the phone distracted him from these musings. It was his sister Jasmina, calling him to say that Britt had decided not to wait until the morning to travel into the desert, but with all the confidence of someone who believed she knew the wilderness—every wilderness—Britt had insisted on setting out by road, just a couple of hours ago.

Issuing a clipped goodbye to his sister, he went into action. No wonder he'd felt apprehensive. Here with tents erected against the shield of a rock face people were safe, but if the weather worsened out in the desert, and Britt was lost—

All thoughts of Britt in connection with the harem tent shot from his mind. She knew *her* wilderness, not his!

Striding back into the centre of the camp, he was already securing the headdress called a *howlis* around his face and calling for his horse, while his faithful people, seeing that he meant to leave the camp, were gathering round him. They had no time to lose. If a sandstorm was coming, as he suspected, and Britt was alone on treacherously shifting sand, all the technology of a modern age wouldn't save her.

Calling for a camel to carry the equipment he might need, he strode on towards the corral where they were saddling his stallion. Springing onto its back, he took the lead rope from the camel and lashed it to his tack. He wasted no time riding away from the safety of the camp at the head of his small troupe, into what Britt would imagine was the most beautiful and tranquil starlit night.

Where had the romance of the desert gone? She had almost been blasted away in a gust of sand in a last attempt to change the tyre. What was it about her and tyres? And this wasn't fun, Britt concluded, raking her hand across the back of her neck. Sand was getting everywhere. Eddies of sand were exfoliating her face while more sand was slipping through the smallest gap in her clothes.

Did she even stand a chance of being found? Britt wondered, gazing around, really frightened now. Visibility was shrinking to nothing as the wind blew the sand about, and the sky was black. She couldn't even see the stars. She had never felt more alone, or so scared. Battling against the wind, she made it to the back of the Jeep and locked her tools away. Shielding her eyes, she opened the driver's door and launched herself inside. The wind was so strong now it was lifting the Jeep and threatening to turn it over. She had never wished for Sharif more. She couldn't care less about their differences right now. She just wanted him to find her.

She had checked the weather before setting out, but could never have imagined how quickly it could change. There was nothing to see out of the window. She changed her mind about Sharif finding her. It was too dangerous. She didn't want him to risk his life. But she just couldn't sit here, helpless, waiting to buried, or worse… She had to remain visible. If the Jeep were buried she would never be found.

There was a warning triangle in the boot—and a spade handle. And the very last thing she needed right now was a bra. She could make a warning symbol. And there were flares in the boot.

Downside? She would just have to brave the storm again.

The wind was screaming louder than ever and the sand was like an industrial rasp. But she was determined—determined to live, determined to be seen, and determined to do everything in her power to ensure that happened.

Once she had managed to get everything out of the back of the Jeep, securing the warning triangle to the handle of the spade with her bra was the easy part. Finding a way to fix it onto the Jeep wasn't quite so simple. She settled for wedging it into the bull bars, and now she had to get back into the shelter of the vehicle as quickly as she could or she would be buried where she stood.

Closing the door, she relished the relative silence, and, turning everything off, she resigned herself to the darkness. She had to conserve power. There was nothing more she could do for now but wait out the storm and hope that when it passed over she would still be alive and could dig her way out.

CHAPTER TEN

DISMOUNTING, SHARIF COVERED his horse's face with a cloth so he could lead it forward. Attached to his horse by a rope was the camel loaded down with equipment. The camel's eyelashes provided the ultimate in protection against the sand, while he had to be content with narrowing his eyes and staring through the smallest slit in his *howlis*. His men had gathered round him, and so long as he could see the compass he was happy he could lead them to Britt's Jeep. When all else failed magnetic north saved the day.

As they struggled on against the wind he sent up silent thanks that Jasmina had been able to text him Britt's last coordinates, but a shaft of dread pierced him when he wondered if he would reach her in time.

He *had* to reach her in time. He had intended to test Britt as she had tested him in Skavanga when she arrived in the desert, but not like this.

What would she think when he appeared out of the storm? That a bandit was coming for her? It only occurred to him now that she had never seen him in robes before. That seemed so unimportant. He just prayed he would find her alive. He had left the encampment battening down for what was essentially a siege. Custom dictated the tribe pitch their tents at the foot of a rock face to allow for situations like a sandstorm. The best he could hope for where Britt was concerned was that she'd had enough sense to stay inside her vehicle. She wouldn't stand a cat in hell's chance outside.

The scream of the wind was unbearable. It seemed never ending. It was as if a living creature were trying every way it knew how to reach her inside the Jeep. Curled up defensively with her hands over her ears, she knew that the electrics were shot and the phone was useless. The sand was already halfway up the window. How much longer could she survive this?

What a rotten end, she thought, grimacing at the preposterous situation in which she found herself. She could only feel sorry for the person who had to drag her lifeless body out of the Jeep—

She Would Not Die Like This.

Throwing her weight against the driver's door, she tried to force it open, but it wouldn't budge—and even if it had, where was she going?

Flares were her last hope, Britt reasoned. She had no idea now if it was day or night, and before she could set off a flare she needed something to break the window.

Climbing over the seats, she found everything she needed. The vehicle was well equipped for a trek in the desert. There were flares and work gloves, safety goggles, a hard hat, and heavy-duty cutters, as well as a torch and a first-aid kit. Perfect. She was in business.

He had almost given up hope when he saw the flare flickering dimly in the distance. Adrenalin shot through his veins, giving him the strength of ten men and the resolve of ten more. He urged his weary animals on and his brave men followed close behind him. He couldn't be sure it was Britt who had let off the flare until he saw the warning triangle she had fixed onto the top of a spade handle with a bra, and then he smiled. Britt was ever resourceful, and any thought he might have had about her setting off into the desert at night without a proper guide seemed irrelevant as he forged on, his lungs almost exploding as he strained against the wind. Nothing could keep him back. Sharp grains of sand whirled around him, but the robes protected him and the *howlis* did its job. Just thinking about Britt and how frightened she must be made his discomfort irrelevant. His only goal was to reach her—to save her—to protect her—to somehow get her back to the camp—

If she were still alive.

He prayed that she was, as he had never prayed before. He prayed that he could save her as he sprang down from his horse, and started to work his way around the buried Jeep. The vehicle was buried far deeper than he had imagined, and, worse, he couldn't hear anything against the wind. Was she alive in there? With not a moment to lose he yanked at the windscreen with his men helping him. Britt had already loosened it to let off the flare—

And then he saw her. Alive! Though clearly unconscious. She had managed to free the rubber seal on the glass and had forced it out far enough to let off the flare, but in doing so had allowed sand to pour in and fill the vacuum, almost burying her. He waved his men back. It wasn't safe. Too many of them and the Jeep might sink further into the sand or even turn over on top of them, killing his men and burying Britt. He would not let anyone else take the risk of pulling her out.

He dug with his hands, and with the spade he had freed from the bull bars of the Jeep. He was desperate to reach her—frantic to save her. It was the longest hour of his life, and also his greatest triumph when he finally sliced through Britt's seat belt with the *khanjar* at his side, and lifted her to safety in his arms.

To say she was bewildered would be putting it mildly. She had woken up to find herself transported from a nightmare into a Hollywood blockbuster, complete with sumptuous Arabian tent and billowing curtains, with not a grain of sand to be seen. Added to which, there were women clustering around what passed for her bed. Dressed in rainbow hues, they looked amazing with their flowing gowns and veils. At the moment they were trying to explain to her in a series of mimes that she had been barely conscious when their leader carried her into the camp. At which point it seemed they had to pause and sigh.

She must have been asleep for ages, Britt realised, staring around. The bed on which she was reclining was covered in the most deliciously scented cushions, and was enclosed by billowing white curtains, which the women had drawn back. She felt panicked for a moment as she tried to take it all in. Was this the encampment Jazz had told her about—or was she somewhere else?

And then it all came flooding back. The terrifying storm— The sickening fear of being buried alive. Her desperate attempt to set off a flare, not knowing if anyone would see it—

Someone had. She squeezed out a croak on a throat that felt as if it had been sandpapered, and the women couldn't understand a word she said, anyway, so the identity of her rescuer was destined to remain a mystery.

The women were instantly sympathetic and rushed to bring her drinks laced with honey, and one of them indicated an outdoor spa, which Britt could now see was situated at the far end of the tent.

And what a tent! It was more of a pavilion, large and lavishly furnished with colourful hangings and jewel-coloured rugs covering the floor. Burnished brass lanterns decorated with intricate piercing cast a soft golden glow, while the roof was gathered up in the centre and had been used to display a number of antique artefacts. She was still staring up in wonder when the women distracted her. They had brought basins of cool water and soft towels, and, however much she indicated that she could sort herself out, they insisted on looking after her and bathing all her scratches and battle wounds.

It was a nice feeling to be made so welcome. Thanking the women with smiles, she drank their potions and accepted some of their tiny cakes, but she couldn't lie here all day like some out-of-work concubine. She was badly in need of a sugar rush to kick her into gear. And those little cakes were delicious. She was contentedly munching when she suddenly remembered Jazz. Sharif's sister must be out of her mind with worry—

Thank goodness she had a signal. She quickly stabbed in: *safe @camp. sorry if i frightnd u! lost a day sleeping! talk soon* J

A message came back before she had chance to put the phone away: *relieved ur safe. Look fwd 2 mtg u b4 long!* ☺

Britt smiled as she put the phone down again. She looked forward to that meeting too. And now the women were miming that she should come with them. She hesitated until they pointed towards the spa again, but the thought of bathing in clean, warm water was irresistible.

She was a little concerned when the women started giggling as they drew her out of the bed and across the rugs towards the bathing pool, especially when they started giggling and then sighing in turn. Were they preparing her for the sheikh? Was she to be served up on a magic carpet with a honey bun in her mouth?

Not if she could help it.

She asked with gestures: 'Did your sheikh bring me here?' She tried to draw a picture with her hands of a man who was very tall and robed, which was about all she could remember of her rescuer—that and his black horse. She must have kept slipping into unconsciousness when he brought her back here. 'The Black Sheikh?' she suggested, gazing around the golden tent, hoping to find something black to pounce on. 'His Majesty, Sheikh Sharif al Kareshi…?'

The women looked at her blankly, and then she had an idea. She sighed theatrically as they had done.

Exclaiming with delight, they smiled back, nudging each other as they exchanged giggles and glances.

She left a pause to allow for more sighs while her heart thundered a blistering tattoo. So it was very likely that Emir or Sharif, or whatever he was calling himself these days, had rescued her. Her brain still wasn't functioning properly, but it seemed preferable to be in the tent of someone she knew, even if that someone was the Black Sheikh.

She allowed the women to lead her into the bathing pool. She didn't want to offend them and what was the harm of refreshing herself so she could start the new day and explore the camp? The women were keen to pamper her outer self with unguents, and her inner self with fresh juice. One of them played a stringed instrument softly in the background, while the scent rising from the warm spring water was divine. Relaxing back in the clear, warm water, she indulged in a little dream in which she was a young woman lost in the desert who had been rescued by a handsome sheikh—

She *was* a young woman lost in the desert who had been rescued by a handsome sheikh!

And however she felt about him, the first thing she had to do was thank Sharif for saving her life. She had to forget all about who had done what to whom, or how angry she had been about his people's interference in the business, and start with that. She could always tell him what she thought about his high-handed ways afterwards. Sharif had risked his life to save her. Compared to that, her pride counted for nothing.

The women interrupted her thoughts, bringing her towels, which they held out like a screen so she could climb from the pool with her modesty intact. They quickly wrapped her, head to foot, and she noticed now that the sleeping area had already been straightened, and enough food to feed an army had been laid out.

Was she expecting visitors?

One visitor?

Her heart thundered at the thought.

As they led her towards the bed of cushions she caught sight of the lavender sky, tinged with the lambent gold of a dying sun. The women insisted she must lie down on a sheet while they massaged her skin with soothing emollients to ease the discomfort of all the cuts and bruises she had sustained during her ordeal. The scent of the cream was amazing and she couldn't ever remember being indulged to this extent. Being prepared for the sheikh indeed...

She was a little concerned when, instead of her own clothes, the women showed her an exquisite gown in flowing silk. 'Where are my clothes?' she mimed.

One of the women mimed back that Britt's clothes were still wet after having been washed.

Ah... 'Thank you.'

She bit her lip, wondering how the rest of this night would play out, but then decided she would just have to throw herself into the spirit of generosity being lavished on her by these wonderful people. And the gown was beautiful, though it had clearly been designed for someone far more glamorous than she was. In ice blue silk, it was as fine as gossamer, and was intricately decorated with silver thread. It was the sort of robe she could easily imagine a sheikh's mistress wearing. But as there were no alternatives on offer...

One of the women brought in a full-length mirror so Britt could see the finished effect. The transformation was complete when they draped a matching veil over her hair and drew the wisp of chiffon across her face, securing it with a jewelled clip. She stood for a moment staring at her reflection in amazement. At least she fitted in with the surroundings now, and for perhaps the first time ever she felt different about herself and didn't long for jeans or suits. She had never worn anything so exotic, or believed she had the potential to project an air of mystery. I could be the Sheikh's diamond, she thought with amusement.

She tensed as something changed in the tent...a rustle of cloth...a hint of spice...

She turned to find the women backing away from her.

And then she saw the man. Silhouetted with his back against the light, he was tall and powerful and dressed in black robes. A black headdress covered half his face, but she would have known him anywhere, and her body yearned for her lover before her mind had chance to make a reasoned choice.

'So it was you…' Even as she spoke she realised how foolish that must sound.

His Majesty, Sheikh Sharif al Kareshi, the man known to the world as the Black Sheikh, and known to her before today as Emir, loosened his headdress. Every thought of thanking him for saving her life, or condemning him for walking out on her without explaining why, faded into insignificance as their stares met and held.

'Thank you for saving my life,' she managed on a throat that felt as tight as a drum.

She was mad with herself. The very last thing she had intended when she first set out on this adventure was to be in awe of Sharif. She had come to rail at him, to demand answers, but now she was lost for words and all that seemed to matter was that they were together again. 'You risked your life for me—'

'I'm glad to see you up and well,' he said, ignoring this. Removing his headdress fully, he cast the yards of heavy black silk aside.

'I am very well, thanks to you.'

Dark eyes surveyed her keenly. 'Do you have everything you need?'

As Sharif continued to hold her stare her throat seemed to close again. She felt horribly exposed in the flowing, flimsy gown and smoothed her hands self-consciously down the front of it.

'Relax, Britt. We're the same people we were in Skavanga.'

Were they? Just hearing his voice in these surroundings seemed so surreal.

'You've had a terrible ordeal,' he pointed out. 'Why don't you make the most of this break?'

'Your Majesty, I—'

'Please—' he stopped her with the hint of a smile '—call me Sharif.' He paused, and then added, 'Of course, if you prefer, you can call me Emir.'

The laughter in his eyes was quickly shuttered when she drew herself up. 'There are many things I'd like to call you, but Emir isn't one of them,' she assured him. 'This might not be the time to air grievances—after all, you did save my life—'

'But you're getting heated,' he guessed.

'I am curious to know why you found it necessary to deceive me.'

'I conduct my business discreetly.'

'Discretion's one thing—deception's another.'

'I never deceived you, Britt.'

'You didn't explain fully, did you? I still don't know why you left in such a hurry.'

'Things moved faster than I expected, and I wasn't in a position to explain them to you.'

'The Black Sheikh is held back? By whom?'

'I'm afraid I can't tell you that.'

'Isn't that taking loyalty too far?'

'Loyalty can never be taken too far,' Sharif assured her. 'Just be satisfied that your sisters were not involved and that everything I've done has been for the sake of the company—'

'And your deal.'

'Obviously, the consortium is a consideration.'

'I bet,' she muttered. 'I'm glad you find this amusing,' she added, seeing his eyes glinting.

'I don't find it in the least amusing. When a company defaults on a payment risking the livelihoods of families who have worked for Skavanga Mining for generations, I did what I could to put things right as fast as I could, and while you were still in the air flying to Kareshi to see me.'

She knew this was true and blushed furiously beneath her veil. She was used to being on top of things—at work and with her sisters. She was also used to being told all the facts, and yet Sharif was holding something back for the sake of loyalty, he had implied—but loyalty to whom?

It hardly mattered. He wasn't going to tell her, Britt realised with frustration. 'Okay, I'm sorry. Maybe I did overreact, but it still doesn't explain why you couldn't have said something before you left the cabin.'

'I'm not in the habit of explaining myself to anyone.'

'You don't say,' she murmured.

'It's just how I am, Britt.'

'Accountable to no one,' she guessed.

The Black Sheikh dipped his head.

'Well, whatever you've done, or haven't done, thank you—' She was on the point of thanking him again for saving her life, when Sharif held up his hands.

'Enough, Britt. You don't have to say it again.' Glancing towards the curtained sleeping area, he added, 'And you should take a rest.'

Her mind had been safely distracted from the sumptuous sleeping area up to now, and she stepped back, unconsciously putting some distance between herself and Sharif. She needed time to get her thoughts in order. Better do something mundane, she decided, drawing back the curtains. Task completed, she turned to face Sharif, who made her the traditional Kareshi greeting, touching his chest, his mouth and finally his brow.

'It means peace,' he said dryly. 'And you really don't have to stand in my presence, Britt.'

'Maybe I prefer to—'

'And maybe, as I suggested, you should take a rest.'

Now was not the time to argue, so she compromised, sitting primly on the very edge of one of the deep, silk-satin cushion. 'I apologise for putting you to so much trouble,' she said, gesturing around. 'I had no idea a storm was coming, or that it would close in so quickly. I did do my research—'

'But you couldn't wait to come and see me a moment longer?' he suggested dryly.

'It wasn't like that.' It was like that, Britt admitted silently.

She watched warily as Sharif prowled around the sleeping area, his prayer beads clicking at his waist in a constant reminder that she was well out of her comfort zone here. She stiffened when he came to sit with her—on the opposite side of the cushions, true, but close enough to set her heart racing. And while she was dressed in this flimsy gown, a style that was so alien to her in every way, she couldn't help feeling vulnerable.

'The women gave me this gown to wear while they were washing my clothes,' she felt bound to explain.

'Very nice,' he said.

Very nice was an understatement. The gown was gloriously feminine and designed to seduce—which she could have done without right now. Her sisters would laugh if they could see her. Britt Skavanga backed into a corner, and now lost for words.

CHAPTER ELEVEN

'I AM GLAD you have been given everything you need,' Sharif said, glancing round the sumptuous pavilion.

'Everything except my clothes.' Britt was becoming increasingly aware that the gown the women had dressed her in was almost sheer. 'I believe my own clothes will soon be here.' She had no idea when they were arriving, or even if they would ever arrive. She only knew that her body burned beneath Sharif's stare as his lazy gaze roved over the diaphanous gown—she had never longed for a business suit more.

Sharif's lips tugged a little at one corner as if he knew this.

Turning away, she ground her teeth with frustration at the position she found herself in. Of course she was grateful to Sharif for saving her, but being housed in the harem at the sheikh's pleasure was hardly her recreation of choice—

She had to calm down and accept that a lot had happened in the past twenty-four hours and she was emotionally overwrought. The temptation to do exactly as Sharif suggested—relax and recline, as he was doing—was overwhelming, but with his familiar, intoxicating scent washing over her—amber, patchouli and sandalwood, combined with riding leather and clean, warm man—she couldn't be answerable for her own actions if she did that. Business was her safest option. 'If I'd seen a photograph of you before you came to Skavanga, I wouldn't have mixed you up with Emir and maybe we could have avoided this mess, and then you wouldn't have been forced to risk your life riding through the storm to find me.'

'I don't make a habit of issuing photographs with business letters. And as it happens, I did see a photograph of you, but it wasn't a true representation.'

'What do you mean?' she asked.

'I mean the photograph showed one woman when you are clearly someone very different.'

'In what way?'

Sharif smiled faintly. 'You're far more complex than your photograph suggests.'

She pulled a face beneath the veil, remembering the posed shot. She had been wearing a stiff suit and an even stiffer expression. She hated having her photograph taken, but had been forced to endure that one for the sake of the company journal.

'Well, I haven't seen a single photograph of you in the press,' she countered.

'Really?' Sharif pretended concern. 'I must remedy that situation immediately.'

'And now you're mocking me,' she protested.

He shrugged. 'I thought we agreed to call a truce. But if there's nothing more you need—'

'Nothing. Thank you,' she said stiffly as he turned to go. Her body, of course, had other ideas. If she could just keep her attention fixed on something apart from Sharif's massive shoulders beneath his flowing black robe, or those strong tanned hands that had given her so much pleasure—

'I'll leave you to rest,' he said, getting up.

'Thank you.'

And now she was disappointed?

He was leaving while her body was on fire for him.

Yes. And she should be glad, Britt told herself firmly. A heavy pulse might be throbbing between her legs, but this man was not Emir—and Emir had been dangerous enough—this man was a regal and unknowable stranger, who could pluck her heart from her chest and trample it underfoot while she was still in an erotic daze. She stood too and, lifting her chin, she directed a firm stare into his eyes. Even that was a mistake. Lust ripped through her, along with the desire to mean something to this man. For a few heady seconds she could think of nothing but being held by him, kissed by him, and then, thankfully, she pulled herself round.

'This is wonderful accommodation and I can't thank you enough for all you've done for me. Your people are so very kind. They let me sleep, they tended to my wounds, they—'

'They bathed you?' Sharif supplied.

The way his mouth kicked up at one corner sent such a vivid flash of sensation ripping through her she almost forgot what she was going to say. 'I...I had a bath,' she admitted in a shaking voice that was not Britt Skavanga at all.

'They spoiled you with soothing emollients, and that's so bad?'

'They did,' she agreed, wishing he would look anywhere but into her eyes with that dark, mocking stare. And every time she nodded her head, tiny jewels tinkled in a most alluring way—she could do without that too!

'The women have dressed you for their sheikh,' Sharif observed.

And now she couldn't tell if he was joking or not. Her chest was heaving with pent-up passion thanks to her desire deep down to be angry—to have a go. *He can't talk to you like that!* She wasn't a canapé to whet his appetite—a canapé carefully prepared and presented to the sheikh for him to sample, then either swallow or discard.

'They have prepared you well,' Sharif said, showing not the slightest flicker of remorse for this outrageous statement. 'Would you rather they had brought you something ugly to wear?' he demanded when her body language gave away her indignation. 'Moral outrage doesn't suit you, Britt,' he went on in the same mocking drawl. 'It's far too late for that. But I must say the gown suits you. That shade of blue is very good with your eyes…'

So why wasn't he looking into her eyes?

Straightening up, she wished her jeans and top were dry so she could bring an end to this nonsense.

And yet…

And yet she was secretly glad that Sharif's gaze was so appreciative. Why else would she stand so straight? Why were her lips parted, and why was she licking them with the tip of her tongue? And why, for all that was logical, was she thrusting her breasts out when her nipples were so painfully erect?

'It's a very pretty dress,' she agreed coolly.

'Our desert fashions suit you,' Sharif agreed.

She shivered involuntarily as he reached out to run the tip of his forefinger down the very edge of her veil. There was still a good distance between them, but no distance could be enough.

And now her thoughts were all erotic. Perhaps Sharif saving her life had added a primitive edge to her feelings towards him. The desire to thank him fully, and in the most obvious way, was growing like a madness inside her. Thank goodness for the veil.

'I'll call back later—when you've had a rest,' he said.

She watched without saying anything as Sharif drew the gauzy curtains around the sleeping area. She reminded herself firmly that she might be dressed like the sugar plum fairy, but she had no intention of dancing to his tune. She was here for business, and business alone. She had to be wary of this man. Sharif had spoken to her sisters without telling her. He had taken mineral samples from the mine, and yet he hadn't had the courtesy to share the results of the tests with her. This might be a seductive setting, she reasoned angrily as the curtains around the sleeping area blew in the warm, early evening breeze, and Sharif was certainly the most seductive of men, but, grateful or not, she still wanted answers, and he had a lot of explaining to do.

He was back? She tried not to care—not to show she cared. She must have failed miserably as breath shot out of her when he dragged her close. This was not even the civilised businessman—this was the master of the desert. There was no conversation between them, no debate. And there was quite definitely no thought of business in Sharif's eyes. There was just the determination to master her and share her pleasure.

'Well, Britt?' Sharif demanded, holding her in front of him. 'You had enough to say for yourself in Skavanga. You must have something to say to me now. Why did you really come to Kareshi when you could have wired your test results and I could have done the same? When you could have laid out your complaints against me in an email message without making this trip?'

Why had she listened to Eva? Eva was hot-headed

and impetuous, and was always getting herself into
some sort of trouble, while Britt was cool and meticulous, and never allowed emotion to get in the way.

How had this happened?

'Why are you really here?' Sharif pressed mercilessly, smiling grimly down into her eyes. 'What do
you need from me?'

He knew very well what she needed from him. She
needed his hands on her body, and his eyes staring deep
into hers. She needed his scent and heat to invade her
senses, and his body to master hers—

His senses raged as Britt pressed her body against his.
This was his woman. This was the woman he remembered and desired. This was the fierce, driven woman
he had first met in Skavanga, the woman who took
what she wanted and rarely thought about it afterwards.

'Sharif?'

Could it be possible that he didn't want that part of
her? he marvelled as Britt spoke his name. Did that
wildcat bring out the worst in him? Loosening his grip
on her arms, he let her go. When he had first entered the
pavilion he had seen the tender heart of a woman he had
started to know in Skavanga—the vulnerable woman
inside the brittle shell—the woman he had walked away
from before he could cause her any hurt.

'Sharif, what is it?'

He stared down and saw the disappointment in her
eyes. And why shouldn't Britt expect the worst when
he had walked out on her before?

Everything had been so cut and dried in the past.
He'd fed his urges and moved on, but he had never
met a woman like this before. He had never realised a
woman could come to mean so much to him. The feel-

ings raging inside him when he had found Britt alive
were impossible to describe. All he could think was:
she was still in the world, and thank God for it. But he
had a country to rule and endless responsibilities. Did
he make love to her now, as he so badly wanted to do,
or did he save her by turning and walking away?

'It's not like you to hesitate,' she murmured.

'And it's not like you to be so meek and mild,' he
countered with an ironic smile. 'What shall we do about
this role reversal?'

'You're asking me?' she queried, starting to smile.

He closed his eyes, allowing her scent and warmth
and strength to curl around his core, clearing his mind.
He prided himself on his self-control, but there was will
power and then there was denial, and he wasn't in the
mood to deny either of them tonight. He wanted Britt.
She wanted him. It was that simple. Above all, he was
a sensualist who never ate merely because he was hungry, but only when the food was at its best. Britt thought
she knew everything about men and sex and satisfaction, but it would be his pleasure to teach her just how
wrong she was.

'What are you doing?' she said as he led her back
through the billowing curtains.

Settling himself on the silken cushions, he raised a
hand and beckoned to her.

'What the hell do you think this is?' she said.

'This is a harem,' he said with a shrug. 'And if you
don't like that idea you might want to step out of the
light.'

'I'll stand where I like,' she fired back.

His shrugged again as if to say that was okay with
him. It was. There wasn't one inch of Britt that wasn't
beautifully displayed or made even more enticing by

the fact that she was wearing such an ethereal gown and standing in front of the light. He let the silence hang for a while, and then, almost as if it were an afterthought, he said, 'When the women brought that gown, didn't they bring you any underwear?'

Her gasp of outrage must have been heard clearly in Skavanga.

'You are totally unscrupulous,' she exclaimed, wrapping the flimsy folds around her.

'I meant no offence,' he said, having difficulty hiding his grin as he eased back on the cushions. 'I was merely admiring you—'

'Well, you can stop admiring me right now.'

'Are you sure about that?'

'Yes, I'm sure. I feel ridiculous—'

'You look lovely. Now, come over here.'

'You must be joking.'

'So stand there all night.'

'I won't have to,' she said confidently, 'because at some point you'll leave. At which time I will settle down to sleep on *my* bed.'

Britt looked magnificent when she was angry. Proud and strong, and finely bred, she reminded him of one of his prized Arabian ponies. And this was quite a compliment coming from him. Plus, a little teasing was in order. Hadn't she put him through trials by fire and ice in Skavanga? Britt had done everything she could think of to unsettle him while he was on her territory, but now the tables were turned she didn't like it. 'Come on,' he coaxed. 'You know you want to—'

'I know I don't,' she flashed. 'Just because you saved my life doesn't give you droit de seigneur!'

'Ah, so you're a virgin,' he said as if this were news to him. 'When did that happen?'

Her look would have felled most men. It suggested she would like to bring the curtains and even the roof down on his head. She was so sure he had styled himself on some sheikh of old, she couldn't imagine that beneath his robes he was the same man she had met in Skavanga. He should get on with proving that he was that man, but he was rather enjoying teasing her. Helping himself to some juice and a few grapes, he left Britt to draw back a curtain to scan the tent, no doubt searching for another seating area. She wouldn't find one, and he had no intention of going anywhere.

'There's nowhere else to sit,' she complained. 'Until you go,' she added pointedly.

He shrugged and carried on eating his grapes. 'Formal chairs are not required in the harem—so there is just this all-purpose sleeping, lounging, pleasuring area, where I'm currently reclining.'

'Don't remind me! I don't know what game you're playing, Sharif, but I'd like you to leave right now.'

'I'm not going anywhere. This is my camp, my pavilion, my country—and you,' he added with particular charm, 'are my guest.'

'I treated you better than this when you were my guest.'

He only had to raise a brow to remind Britt that she had treated him like a fool, and was surprised when he had turned the tables on her at the lake.

'I came to do business with you,' she protested, shifting her weight from foot to foot—doing anything rather than sit with him. 'If you had stuck around long enough for us to have a proper discussion in Skavanga, I wouldn't even be here at all.'

'So that's what this is about,' he said. 'It still hurts.'

'You bet it does.'

He had left at the right time and, though he wouldn't betray Tyr's part in the business, he wanted to reassure her. 'Well, I'm sorry,' he said. 'It seems I must learn to explain myself in future.'

'Damn right you should,' she said, crossing her arms.

'I'm just so glad you're here—and in one piece.'

'Thank you for reminding me,' she said wryly. 'You know I can't be angry with you now.'

They were both in the same difficult place. They wanted each other. They both understood that if you laid the bare facts on the table theirs was not a sensible match. The only mistake that either of them had made was wanting more than sex out of this relationship.

'So maybe we can be friends?' she said as if reading his mind. 'Except in business, of course,' she added quickly.

'Maybe,' he said. 'Maybe business too.'

After a long pause, she said, 'So, tell me about the tent. Do your people always provide you with a harem tent—just in case?'

'In case of what?' he prompted, frowning.

'I think you know what I mean—'

'Come and sit with me so I can tell you about it. Or don't you trust yourself to sit close to me?' he added, curbing his smile.

She chose a spot as far away from him as possible. Again he was reminded of his finely bred Arabian ponies, whose trust must be earned. Britt was as suspicious as any of them. 'Remember the deer,' he said.

'The deer?' she queried.

'Remember the deer in Skavanga and how relaxed we were as we watched them?'

'And then you'll tell me about the tent?'

'And then I'll tell you about the tent,' he promised.

She hardly knew Sharif, and they sat in silence until—yes, she remembered the deer—yes, she began to relax.

'This pavilion is a priceless artefact,' he said. 'Everything you see around you has been carefully preserved—and not just for years, but for centuries by the people in this camp and by their ancestors. It is a treasure beyond price.'

'Go on,' she said, leaning forward.

'You may have guessed from the lack of seating that this pleasure tent is devoted to pursuits that allow a man or a woman to take their ease. Pleasure wasn't a one-sided affair for the sheikhs. Many women asked to be considered for the position of concubine.'

'More fool them.'

'What makes you say that?' he asked as she removed the veil from her hair.

She huffed. 'Because I would never be seduced so easily.'

'Really?'

'Really.'

'It's a shame your nipples are such a dead giveaway.'

She looked down quickly and, after blushing furiously, she had to laugh.

'Shall I go on?'

'Please…'

'After yet another day of struggles beneath the merciless sun,' he declaimed as if standing in an auditorium, 'fighting off invaders—hunting for food—the sheikh would return…'

'Drum roll?'

He laughed. 'If you like.'

'How many women did he return to?'

'At least a football team,' he teased. 'Maybe more.'

'Sheikhs must have been pretty fit back then.'

'Are you suggesting I'm not?'

She met his eyes and smiled and he thought how attractive she was, and how overwhelmingly glad he would always be that he'd found her in time to save her. He went on with his storytelling. 'Or, maybe there could be just one special woman. If she pleased the sheikh one woman would be enough.'

'Lucky her!' Britt exclaimed. 'Until the sheikh decides to increase his collection of doting females, I presume?'

She amused him. And he liked combative Britt every bit as much as her softer self. 'Your imagination is a miraculous thing, Britt Skavanga.'

'Just as well since it allows me to anticipate trouble.'

'So, what's the difference between my story and the way you have treated men in the past? You think of yourself as independent, don't you? You're a woman who does as she pleases?'

'You bet I am.'

'No one forced any of the sheikh's women to enter the harem. They did so entirely of their own accord.'

'And no doubt considered it an honour,' she agreed, flashing him an ironic look.

'But surely you agree that a woman is entitled to the same privileges as a man?'

'Of course I do.'

Where was this leading? Britt wondered. Why did she feel as if Sharif was backing her into a corner? Perhaps it was his manner. He was way too relaxed.

'So if you agree,' he said with all the silky assurance of the desert lion she thought him, 'can you give me a single reason why you shouldn't take your pleasure in the sheikh's pavilion...like a man?'

Her mouth opened and closed again. The only time

she was ever lost for words was with Sharif, Britt realised with frustration. He was as shrewd as he was dis-
tractingly amusing, and was altogether aware of how
skilfully he had backed her into that tight little corner.
He was in fact a pitiless seducer who knew very well
that, where he might have failed to impress her with
the fantasy of the harem tent, with its billowing curtains and silken cushions, or even the rather seductive
clothes they were both wearing, he could very quickly
succeed with fact. She had always been an ardent be-
liever in fact.

CHAPTER TWELVE

SHE COULD HARDLY believe that Sharif had just given her a licence to enjoy him in a room specifically created for that purpose. Crazy. But not without its attraction, Britt realised, feeling her body's eager responses. But she would be cautious. She had heard things about Kareshi. And she liked to be in control. What if she didn't like some of these pleasures Sharif was hinting at? Her gaze darted round. She started to notice things she hadn't seen before. They might be ancient artefacts, as Sharif described them, but they were clearly used for pleasure.

She drew in a sharp, guilty breath hearing him laugh softly. 'Where are you now, Britt?' he said.

Caught out while exploring Planet Erotica, she thought. 'I'm in a very interesting tent—I can see that now.'

'Very interesting indeed,' Sharif agreed mildly, and he made no move to come any closer. 'So I have laid you bare at last, Britt Skavanga?'

'Meaning?' she demanded, clutching the edges of her robe together.

'Have I challenged your stand only to find it has been erected on dangerously shifting sand?' Sharif queried with a dangerous glint in his eyes. 'I've offered you the freedom of the harem—the opportunity to take your pleasure like a man—and yet you are hesitating?'

'Maybe you're not as irresistible as you think.'

'And maybe you're not being entirely truthful,' he said. 'What do you see around you, Britt? What do your prejudices lead you to suppose? Do you think that women were brought here by force? Do you look around and see a prison? I look around and see a golden room of pleasure.'

'That's because you're a sensualist and I'm a modern woman who's got more sense.'

'So quick sex in a corner is enough for you?'

'I deplore this sort of thing.'

The corner of Sharif's mouth kicked up. 'You're such a liar, Britt. You have an enquiring mind, and even now you're wondering—'

'Wondering what?'

'Exactly,' he said. 'You don't know.'

'That's no answer to that.'

'Other than to say, you're wondering if there can be pleasure even greater than the pleasure we have already shared. Why don't you find out? Why don't you throw your prejudices away? Why don't you open your mind to possibility and to things we *modern-thinking* people may not have discovered if they hadn't been treasured and preserved by tribes like this.'

'There can't be much that hasn't been discovered yet,' she said, gasping as she snatched her hand away when Sharif touched it.

'Did you feel that?' he said.

Feel it? He had barely touched her and her senses had exploded.

'And this,' he murmured, lightly brushing the back of her neck.

Her shoulders lifted as she gave a shaky gasp. 'What is that? The sensation's incredible. What's happening to me?'

'This is happening to you.' Sharif explained, gesturing towards the golden dish of cream the women had used to massage her skin. 'This so-called magic potion has been passed down through the generations. Not magic,' he said, 'just a particular blend of herbs. Still...'

They had a magical effect, Britt silently supplied. The scratches she had acquired during her ordeal in the desert had already vanished, she realised, studying her skin. She shivered involuntarily as Sharif's hand continued its lazy exploration of the back of her neck, moving through her hair, until she could do no more than close her eyes and bask in the most incredible sensation.

'They put lotion on your scalp as well as on your body, and that lotion is designed to increase sensation wherever it touches.'

And they touched practically every part of her, she remembered, though the women had taken great care to preserve her modesty. She looked at Sharif, and saw the amusement in his eyes. So he thought he'd won again.

She stood abruptly, and became hopelessly entangled in her gown.

'I've heard of veils being used as silken restraints and even as blindfolds,' Sharif remarked dryly, 'but why would you need those when you can tie yourself in knots without help from anyone? Here—let me help you...'

She had no alternative but to rest still as Sharif set about freeing her.

She wasn't prepared for him being so gentle with her, or for her own yearning to receive more of this care. She wanted him—she had always wanted him.

She was still a little tense when he unwound the fine

silk chiffon gown—exposing her breasts, her nipples, her belly, her thighs, with just a wisp of fabric covering the rest of her. She concentrated on sensation, glad that Sharif was in no rush. Everything he did was calculated to soothe and please her. He took time preparing her, which she loved. She loved his lack of haste, and his thoroughness, and knew she could happily enjoy this for hours. Sharif's hands were such delicate instruments of pleasure, and so very knowing where she was concerned.

'And now the rest of you,' he said in a tone of voice that was a husky sedative.

Each application of cream brought her to a higher level of arousal and awareness, so that when he slipped a cushion beneath her hips, she understood for the first time what they were for, and applauded their invention. And when he dipped his hands in the bowl of cream a second time, warming it first between his palms…

And when he touched her…

'Good?' he murmured.

'Do you really need me to answer that?'

And at last he touched her where she was aching for him to touch, but his attention was almost clinical in its brevity.

'Not yet,' he soothed when she groaned in complaint.

He sat back, and she heard him washing his hands in the bowl of scented water and then drying his hands on a cloth. 'You need time to appreciate sensation, and I'm going to give you time, Britt.'

She sucked in a shocked breath. Words failed her. Being on the ball in the office was very different from being…on the sheikh's silken cushions.

'Why confine yourself to once or twice a night?' Sharif said, his eyes alive with laughter.

She didn't know whether to be outraged or in for the journey. When would she ever get another chance like this, for goodness' sake? And with Sharif's dark gaze drawing her ever deeper into his erotic world, and the knowing curve of his mouth reassuring her, there was only one reality for her, and that was Sharif.

'And now you have a job to do,' he said, breaking the dangerous spell. Removing the cushions, he carefully eased her legs down.

'What?' she said, wondering if this was the moment to admit to herself that she would walk on hot coals if that was what it took to have Sharif touch her again.

She followed his gaze to the dish of cream.

Desert robes were intended to come off with the least amount of trouble, Britt discovered as she loosened the laces on the front of Sharif's robe. As it dropped away to reveal his magnificent chest she realised that she might have found the sight of such brute force intimidating had she not known that Sharif was subtle rather than harsh and, above all, blessed with remarkable self-control.

She was glad when he turned on his stomach and stretched out. She wasn't sure she was ready for the whole of naked Sharif just yet. This warrior of the desert was a giant of a man with a formidable physique. Using leisurely strokes, she massaged every part of him, though had to stop herself paying too much attention to his buttocks. They might be the most perfect buttocks she had ever seen on a man, buttocks to mould with your hands—to sink your teeth in—but there was only so much cream to spare, she reflected wryly as he turned. 'Did I say you could move?'

'Continue,' he murmured, settling onto his back.

Okay, so she could do this—and with Sharif watching, if she had to. Hadn't they both seen each other naked in the snow? And was she going to turn her back on Sharif's challenge? Because that was what this was. She had acted big-time girl-around-town, and now he'd called her bluff as she'd called his at the ice lake. He'd come through that with flying colours—flying them high and proud.

How could she ever forget?

She took her time scooping up more cream in her hands and spent ages warming it until she really couldn't put off what had to be done any longer. She began with his chest, loving the sensation as she spread the cream across his warm, firm flesh. She moved on down his arms, right to his fingertips where she spent quite a lot of time lavishing care and attention on hands that were capable of dealing the most extreme pleasure—and gasped with shock when Sharif captured her hands and guided them down. They exchanged a look: his challenging and hers defiant.

He won.

Thank goodness.

Sharif had creamed her intimately and she would do the same for him...

Maybe they both won.

She took her time to make certain that every thick, pulsing inch of him was liberally coated with the cream. She was breathless with excitement at the thought of having all of that inside her—

'So, Britt,' he said, distracting her momentarily. 'You're beginning to see the benefit in delay.'

'And what if I am?' she said carelessly.

'Don't pretend with me,' Sharif warned, stretching out, totally unconcerned by his nudity.

As well he might be, she thought, admiring him in silence.

'So what do you think of my golden room of pleasure?' he demanded.

'Not bad,' she agreed. She'd come across perks in business before, but none like this.

'So you like it?' he said with amusement.

'It's fascinating,' was as far as she was prepared to commit. 'Okay, so it's fabulous,' she admitted when he gave her a look.

'But?' he queried.

'It's got such a vibe of forbidden pleasure—how can anyone be here without feeling guilty?'

'Do you feel guilty?'

Actually, no. The cream was beginning to do its work. 'It's just that this is the sort of place where anything could happen...'

'What are you getting at, Britt?'

Her throat tightened. 'I'd like to hear about all the possibilities,' she said.

And so Sharif told her about the various uses of the hard and soft cushions, and the feathers she had been wondering about. She blushed at his forthright description.

'What about your sauna in Skavanga?' Sharif countered, seeing her reaction to his explanation. 'What about your birch twig switches?'

'They are used for health reasons—to get the blood flowing faster.'

She wasn't going to ask any more questions, because she wasn't sure she was ready to hear Sharif's answers.

'Ice and fire,' he murmured, staring at her.

They held that stare for the longest time while decisions were being made by both of them. Finally, she knelt in front of him, and, reaching up, cupped his face in her hands. That thanks she had intended to give him for saving her life was well overdue. Leaning forward, she kissed him gently on the lips.

Sharif's lips were warm and firm. They could curve with humour or press down in a firm line. Both she loved, but now *she* wanted to both tempt and seduce. She increased the pressure and teased his lips apart with his tongue, but just as she began kissing him more deeply Sharif swung her beneath him and pinned her down.

'All that trouble I've gone to with you, Britt Skavanga,' he complained, smiling against her mouth, 'and all you really want is this—'

She let out a shocked cry as Sharif lodged one powerful leg between her thighs, allowing her to feel just how much he wanted it too.

'All you want is the romance of the desert and the sheikh taking you. Admit it,' he said.

'You are impossible.'

'And you are incredible,' he murmured, drawing her into his arms.

'I do want you,' she admitted, still reluctant to give any ground.

'Well, isn't that convenient?' Sharif murmured. 'Because I want you too.'

This teasing was all the more intense because she knew where it was leading. She knew Sharif wouldn't pull back, and nor would she. Somehow her legs opened wider for him, and somehow she was pulling her knees back and pressing her thighs apart and he was testing her for readiness, and catching inside her—

And she was moving her hips to capture more of him, only to discover that the cream had most definitely done its work. One final thrust of her hips and she claimed him completely. When Sharif took her firmly to the hilt, she lost control immediately. She might have called his name. She might have called out anything. She only knew that when the sensation started to subside he took her over the edge again and again.

They were insatiable. No thrust was too deep or too firm, no pace too fast, or too deliciously slow. Her cries of pleasure encouraged Sharif and he made her greedy for more. He never seemed to tire. He never seemed to tire of drawing out her pleasure, either, and each time was more powerful than the last, until finally she must have passed out from exhaustion.

'Welcome to my world, Britt Skavanga,' was the last thing she heard him say before drifting contentedly off to sleep.

CHAPTER THIRTEEN

HE WATCHED BRITT sleeping, knowing he had been searching for a woman like this all his life. *And now he'd found her, he couldn't have her?* Britt would never agree to be his mistress. And when he married—

When he married?

Yes, Sharif's thoughts where Britt was concerned were every bit as strong as that. Selfishly, he hoped she felt the same way about him. But he had always believed when he married it should be for political reasons, for the good of his country. He'd never been much interested before. His council had pressed him into giving advantageous matches consideration, but he'd never had an appetite for the task. He wanted a woman who excited him—a woman like Britt.

Warm certainty rushed through him as he brushed a strand of hair away from Britt's still-flushed face. He would find a way. The Black Sheikh could always find a way. He would never ask Britt to give up her independence. No one knew better than he that privilege came with a price, and that price was freedom to do as he pleased, but with a woman like Britt anything was possible.

Or, was it? Britt was exceptional and could do great things in life. She deserved the chance to choose her own path, while his was cast in stone. And then there was Skavanga Mining, and all the subterfuge with her brother…

He exhaled heavily as business and personal feelings collided. The consortium needed Britt's expertise in the mining industry as well as her people skills, but would she stay with the company when the consortium took over? She had been running the company up to now, so it would take some fine diplomacy on his part to keep Britt on board. Could he find something to soften the blow for her?

His dilemma was this: while he cared deeply for Britt, his loyalty could only be fixed in one direction, and his was firmly rooted in the consortium.

The phone flashing distracted him. It was Raffa to say he had been forced to move money into Skavanga Mining on the recommendation of their financial analysts. Britt could only see this as another plot, when in fact what Raffa had done had saved the company.

'Our money men are already swarming on Skavanga Mining, and we need you on the ground to reassure everyone that the changes don't mean catastrophe,' Raffa was saying.

'What about Tyr?' And the grand reunion he had been planning for Britt.

'Tyr can't be there—'

'What do you mean, Tyr can't be there?' He cursed viciously. Having Tyr in Skavanga in person would have softened the blow for Britt when she discovered Tyr's golden shares had swung the ownership of the company into the hands of the consortium. But now—how was he going to explain Tyr's absence without betraying Britt's brother as he had promised faithfully not to do?

He had to get back to Skavanga Mining right away to sort this out—and he could only do that without Britt's newly discovered emotions getting in the way, which meant returning to Skavanga without her. Thankfully, his jet was always fuelled. 'I'll be there in fourteen hours,' he said, ending the call.

Glancing at Britt, he knew there was no time to waste, and by the time he had woken her and explained as gently as he could about Tyr coming into the equation it could all be over in Skavanga. This was one emergency she would definitely want to be part of, but it was better if he prepared the ground first, and then sent the jet back for her.

She woke cautiously and her first thought was of Sharif. She didn't want to wake him as it was barely dawn. The first thin sliver of light was just beginning to show beneath the entrance to the tent. She stretched luxuriously, and, still half asleep, reached out to find him...

The empty space at her side required she open one eye. The initial bolt of surprise and disappointment was swiftly replaced by sound reasoning. He must have gone riding. It was dawn. It was quiet. It was the perfect time of day for riding. Groaning with contentment, she rolled over in the bed of soft silken cushions, and, clutching one, nestled her face into it, telling herself that it still held Sharif's faint, spicy scent. He'd held her safe through the night, and the pleasure they'd shared was indescribable. The closeness between them was real, and she was content, a state she couldn't claim very often. This encouraged her to dream that one day they might work side by side to create something special, something lasting, and not just for Skavanga, but for Kareshi too.

She stilled to listen to the muffled sounds of the encampment coming to life for another day. She could hear voices calling somewhere in the distance and cooking vessels clanking against each other, and then there was the gentle pop and fizz of the water in her bathing pool as it bubbled up from its warm underground source. Everything was designed to soothe the senses. Everything was in tune with her sleepy, mellow mood. She wasn't too warm or too cold, and her body felt deliciously well used by a man who made every day a special day, an exciting day.

Yes, she was a contented woman this morning, Britt reflected as she stretched languorously on her silken bed, and she couldn't ever remember feeling that way before—

She jumped up when the phone rang.

'Leila?'

She sat bolt upright. When her younger sister called it was invariably good news. Leila didn't have a grouchy bone in her body and had to be one of the easiest people in the world to get along with, and Britt was bursting to share the news about her growing closeness with Sharif. 'It's so good to hear your voice—'

An ominous silence followed.

'Leila, what's wrong?' Britt realised belatedly that if it was dawn in the desert it was the middle of the night in Skavanga.

'I don't know where to start.' Leila's voice was soft and hesitant. 'We're in trouble. You have to come home, Britt. We need you.'

'Who's in trouble? What's happened?' Britt pressed anxiously. Her stomach took a dive as she waited for Leila to answer.

'The company.'

As Leila's voice tailed away Britt glanced at the empty side of the bed. 'Don't worry, I'm coming straight home.'

She was already off the bed and launching herself through the curtains with her brain in gear. 'Hang on a minute, Leila.' Grabbing a couple of towels from the stack by the pool, she wrapped them around her and ran to the entrance of the pavilion where she saw a passing girl and beckoned her over. Smiling somehow, she gestured urgently for her clothes, before retreating back into the privacy of the pavilion.

'Okay, I'm here,' she reassured her sister. 'So tell me what's going on.'

The pause at the other end of the line might have been a few seconds, but it felt like for ever. 'Leila, please,' Britt prompted.

'The consortium has taken over the company,' Leila said flatly.

'*What?*' Britt reeled back. 'How could they do that? I had the confidence of all the small shareholders before I left.'

'But we don't have enough shares between us to stave off a takeover, and they've bought some more from somewhere.'

'The consortium's betrayed our trust?' Which meant Sharif had betrayed her. 'I don't believe it. You must have got it wrong—'

'I haven't got it wrong,' Leila insisted. 'Their money men are already here.'

'In the middle of the night?'

'It's that critical, apparently.'

While she was in a harem tent in the desert!

Had nothing changed? Had she learned nothing? Sharif had walked away from her again—distracted her again. And this time it all but destroyed her. For a moment she couldn't move, she couldn't think.

'I'm sorry if I shocked you,' Leila said.

Shock?

'I'm sorry that you've had to handle this on your

own,' Britt said, forcing her mind to focus. 'I'll be there just as soon as I can get a flight.'

She had been stupidly taken in, Britt realised. Sharif had betrayed her. By his own admission, nothing was signed off without the Black Sheikh's consent. He must have known about the share deals all along.

'There's one thing I don't get,' she said. 'How can the deal be done when the family holds the majority share-holding? You didn't sell out to him, did you?'

'Not us,' Leila said quietly.

'Who then?'

'Tyr...Tyr has always had more shares than we have. Don't you remember our grandmother leaving him the golden shares?'

Shock hit her again. Their grandmother had done something with the shares, Britt remembered, but she had been too young to take it in. 'Is Tyr with you? Is he there?' Suddenly all that mattered was seeing her brother again. Tyr had always made things right when they were little— Or was that just her blind optimism at work again? She couldn't trust her own judgement these days.

'No. Tyr's not here, Britt. Neither Eva or I has seen him. The only thing I can tell you is that Tyr and the Black Sheikh are the main forces behind this deal,' Leila explained, hammering another nail into the coffin of Britt's misguided dream. 'The sheikh has got his law-yers and accountants swarming all over everything.'

'He didn't waste any time,' Britt said numbly. While she had been in bed with Sharif, he had been seeing the deal through and speaking to her brother. This had to be the ultimate betrayal, and was why Sharif hadn't been at her side when she woke this morning. He was already on his way to Skavanga. What could she say to Leila— to either of her sisters? Sorry would never cover it.

'It's such a shock,' Leila was saying. 'We still can't believe this is happening.'

There was no point regretting things that couldn't be changed, Britt reasoned as she switched quickly to reassuring her sister. 'Don't worry about any of this, Leila. Just stay out of it until I get back. I'll handle it.'

'What about you, Britt?'

'What about me?' She forced a laugh. 'Let me go and pack my case so I can come home.'

She had been betrayed by her feelings, Britt realized as she ended the call. She was to blame for this, no one else. And now it was up to her to make things right.

She spun around as the tent flap opened, but her hammering heart could take a break. It was the smiling women with her clothes. And whatever type of man their master was, these women had been nothing but kind to her. Greeting them warmly, she explained with mime that although she would love to spend more time with them, she really couldn't today.

It was as if she had never been away, Britt reflected as the cab brought her into the city from the airport. But had the streets always been so grey? The pavements were packed with ice and with low grey cloud overhead everything seemed greyer than ever. After the desert, she reasoned. This was her home and she loved it whatever the climate might be. This harsh land was where she had been born and bred to fight and she wasn't about to turn tail and run just because the odds were against her. Nothing much frightened her, she reasoned as the cab slowed down outside the offices of Skavanga Mining. Only her heart had ever let her down.

Her sisters were waiting for her just inside the glass entrance doors. Whatever the circumstances she was always thrilled to see them. Knowing there was no time to lose, she had come straight to the office from the airport with the intention of getting straight back in the saddle. Thank goodness she'd had a non-crease business suit and stockings in her carry-on bag. She needed all the armour she could lay her hands on.

'Together we stand,' Britt confirmed when they finally pulled apart from their hug.

'Thank God you're here,' Eva said grimly. 'We're overrun by strangers. We have never needed to show a united force more.'

'Not strangers—people from the consortium,' Leila reassured her. 'But he's here,' Leila added gently. 'I just thought you should know.'

'Tyr's here?' Britt's face dropped as she realised from Leila's expression who her sister was talking about. 'You mean Sharif is here,' she said softly. Better she face him now than later, Britt determined, leading her sisters past Reception towards the stairs. 'With his troops,' Eva added as a warning.

Britt made no response. Troops or not, it made no difference to her. She would face him just the same. She could only hope her heart stopped pounding when she did so.

How the hell had he got here ahead of her?

His private jet, of course—

Get your head together fast, Britt ordered herself fiercely. She was strong. She could do this. She had to do this. She had always protected her sisters and the people who worked for Skavanga Mining. That was her role in life.

Without it what was she?

Nothing had changed, she told herself fiercely.

'Don't worry,' she said. 'I can handle this.'

Eva was right. The first-floor lobby was bustling with people Britt didn't know. Sharif's people—the consortium's people—Sharif had moved them in already. Her temper flared at the thought. But she had to keep her cool. She had lost the initiative the moment she allowed her emotions to come into play, and that must never happen again.

So, Tyr definitely wasn't coming. Sharif had tried to persuade him, but now he put his phone away. Their conversation had been typical of the type Sharif had come to expect from the man who was a latter day Robin Hood. If a worthy cause had to be fought Tyr would drop everything and swing into action. He couldn't blame the man, not with everything that was going on in Tyr's life, but his presence here today would have softened the blow for Britt, whose arrival was imminent. Britt's campaign to save the company was on track, but a happy reunion with the brother she hadn't seen for years was not on the cards. So now she would just be bewildered by what she would see as Tyr's betrayal and his.

He pulled away from the window when he saw Britt's cab arrive. However angry she was he had to keep her on board. Skavanga Mining needed her—

He needed her—

He would protect her from further distress the only way he knew how, which was to say nothing about Tyr, just as he had promised, and allow the blame to fall on the ruthless Black Sheikh instead. He would live up to his reputation. Better she hated him than she blamed Tyr for throwing in his lot with the consortium. Tyr had seen it as the only way to save the company in a hurry, and Tyr was right, though Sharif didn't expect Britt to be so understanding; and with Tyr and the other two men in the consortium tied up half a world away, it was up to him to handle the takeover. There had been time to leave a brief message for Britt with the women at the encampment, and he hoped she'd got it. If not he was in for a stormy ride.

'Britt.' He turned the instant she entered the room. His response to her was stronger than ever. She lit up the room—she lit up his life. She forced him to re-evaluate every decision he had ever made, and he always came to the same conclusion. He would never meet another woman like her, but from her expression he guessed she hated him now. 'Wait for me outside,' she told her sisters in a cold voice that confirmed his opinion.

'Are you sure?' the youngest asked anxiously.

'I'm sure,' Britt said without taking her eyes off him.

She looked magnificent—even better than he remembered. A little crumpled from the journey, maybe, but her bearing was unchanged, and that said everything about a woman who didn't know the meaning of defeat. He'd made a serious error leaving her behind in Kareshi. He should have brought her with him and to hell with the consequences. He should have known that Britt was more than ready for whatever she had to face. Her steely gaze at this moment was unflinching.

'Please sit down,' she said, and then she blinked as if remembering that he was in charge now.

'Thank you,' he said, making nothing of it.

Crossing to the boardroom table, he held out the chair for her and heard the slide of silk stockings as she sat down and crossed her legs. He was acutely aware of her scent, of her, but, despite all those highly feminine traits that she was unable to hide, she was ice.

He chose a chair across the table from her. They both

left the chairman's chair empty, though if Britt felt any irony in sitting beneath portraits of her great-grandfather, who had hacked out a successful mining company from the icy wastes with his bare hands, or the father who had pretty much lost the business in half the time it had taken his own father to build it up, she certainly didn't show it. As far as Britt was concerned, it was business as usual and she was in control.

Even now she felt a conflict inside her that shouldn't exist. She had entered the room at the head of her sisters, determined to fight for them to the end. But seeing Sharif changed everything. It always did. The man beneath that formal suit called to her soul, and made her body crave his protective embrace.

So she might be stupid, but she wasn't a child, she told herself impatiently. She was a grown woman, who had learned how to run this company to the best of her ability when it was thrust upon her, whether she wanted it or not. And nothing had changed as far as she was concerned. 'I called the lawyers in on my way from the airport.'

'There's no point in rushing to do that,' he said, 'when I can fill you in.'

'I prefer to deal with professionals,' she said.

He couldn't blame Britt for the bite in her tone. The way that things had worked out here meant she could only feel betrayed by him.

She searched his eyes, and found nothing. What would he find in hers? The same? If her eyes contained only half the anger and contempt she felt for him, then that would have to do for now. She could only hope the hurt and bewilderment didn't show at all.

'I'd be interested to hear your account of things,' she said coldly. 'I believe my brother's involved in some way.' For the first time she saw Sharif hesitate. 'Did you think I wouldn't find out?'

'In an ideal world I would have liked things to take their course so you could get used to the idea of Tyr's involvement. As it was he stepped in to prevent a hostile takeover from any other quarter.'

'And this isn't a hostile takeover?'

'How can it be when Tyr is involved?'

'I wouldn't know since I haven't heard from him.'

'He is still on his travels.'

'So I believe. I heard he took the coward's way out—'

'No one calls your brother a coward in my hearing,' Sharif interrupted fiercely. 'Not even you, Britt.'

Sharif's frown was thunderous and though she opened her mouth to reply something stopped her.

'You realise Tyr and I go back a long way?'

'I don't know all his friends,' she said. 'I still don't,' she added acidly.

Ignoring her barb, Sharif explained that Kareshi was one of the countries Tyr had helped to independence.

'With his mercenaries?' she huffed scathingly.

He ignored this too. 'With your brother's backing I was able to protect my people and save them from tyrants who would have destroyed our country.' He fixed her with an unflinching stare. 'I will never hear a wrong word said against your brother.'

'I understand that from your perspective, my brother has done no wrong. Tyr knows how to help everyone except his own family—'

'You're so wrong,' Sharif cut in. 'And I'm going to tell you why. If Tyr had added his golden shares to those you and your sisters own, the company would still go down. Add those shares to the weight of the consortium and the funds we can provide—not some time in the future, but right now—and you have real power. That's what your brother's done. Tyr has stepped in to save, not just you and your family, but the company and the people who work here.'

'So why couldn't he tell me that himself?'

'It's up to Tyr to explain when he's ready.' Sharif paused as if he would have liked to say something more, but then he just said quietly, 'Tyr's braver than you know.'

She felt as if she had been struck across the face. There was no battle to fight here. It had already been won.

'A glass of water?' Sharif enquired softly.

She passed an angry hand over her eyes, fighting for composure. She felt sick and faint from all the shocks her mind had been forced to accept. The structure of the business had changed—Tyr was involved, but he still wasn't coming home. And mixed into all this were her feelings for this man. It was too much to take in all at once.

Thrusting her chair back, she stood.

Sharif stood too. 'We want to keep you, Britt—'

'I need time—'

'The consortium could use your people skills as well as the mining expertise you have. At least promise me that you'll think about what I've said.'

'Ten minutes,' she flashed, turning from the table. She had to get out of here—now.

One foot in front of the other—how hard could that be?

That might be easy if she didn't know she had let everyone down. She allowed herself to become distracted and everything had changed. The company might have been thrust upon her, but she had given it all she'd got, and had intended to continue doing so for the rest of her working life. So much for that.

Bracing her arms against the sink in the restroom, she hung her head. She couldn't bear to look at her reflection in the mirror. She couldn't bear to see the longing for Sharif in her eyes. Everything he'd said made sense. He wasn't even taking over and booting her out. They wanted her to stay on, he'd said. And she wanted Sharif in every way a woman could want a man. She wanted them to have a proper relationship that wasn't just founded on sex. She had run the gamut of emotions with him, and had learned from it, but this was the hardest lesson of all: the man they called the Black Sheikh would stop at nothing to achieve his goal—even recruiting Britt's long-lost brother, if that got him where he wanted to be. And Sharif didn't even want the part of her she wanted to give, he wanted her people skills. The only way she could survive knowing that was to revert to being the Britt who didn't feel anything.

Sluicing her face down in cold water, she reached for a towel and straightened up. Now she must face the cold man in the boardroom whom she loved more than life itself, and the only decision left for her to make was whether or not she could stay on here and work for Sharif.

She could stay on. She had to. She couldn't abandon the people who worked here, or her sisters. And if that meant her badly bruised heart took another battering, so what? She would just have to return it to its default setting of stone.

CHAPTER FOURTEEN

BRITT RETURNED TO the boardroom to find Sharif pacing. Caught unawares, he looked like a man with the weight of the world on his back. For the blink of an eye she felt sorry for him. Who shared the load with Sharif? When did he get time off? And then she remembered their time in the desert and her heart closed again.

'There is a problem,' he said, holding her stony gaze trapped in his.

'Oh?' She felt for the wall behind her as wasted emotions dragged her down. She could fix her mind all she liked on being tough and determined, and utterly sure about where she wanted this to go, but when she saw him—when she saw those concerns she couldn't know about furrowing his brow and drawing cruel lines down each side of his mouth—she wanted to reach out to him.

She wanted to help him, and, even more than that, she wanted to stand back to back with Sharif to solve every problem they came across, and she wanted him to feel the same way she did.

'I've had to make some changes to my plans.'

'Trouble in Kareshi?' she guessed.

'A troublesome relation who was banished from the kingdom has returned in my absence and is trying to rally support amongst the bullies who still remain. It's

a basic fight between a brighter modern future for all
and a return to the dark days of the past when a privileged few exploited the majority. I must return. I promised my people that they would never be at the mercy
of bullies again, and it's a promise I intend to keep.'

Sharif really did have the weight of the world on his
shoulders. 'What can I do?' Britt said. Whatever had
led them to this place was irrelevant compared to so
many lives in jeopardy.

'I need your agreement to stay on here. I need you
to do my job for me while I'm away. I need you to ease
the transition so that no one worries about change un-
necessarily. Will you do that for me, Britt?'

Sharif needed her. The people here needed her. And
if he didn't need her in the way she had hoped he would,
she still couldn't turn her back on him, let alone turn
her back on the other people she cared about.

'I really need you to do this for me, Britt.'

Her heart hammered violently as Sharif came closer
to make his point, but he maintained some distance
between them, and she respected that. Her heart responded. Her soul responded. She could no more refuse this man than she could turn and walk away from
her duties here. But there was one thing she did have to
know. 'Am I doing this for you, or for the consortium?'

'You're doing it for yourself, and for your people,
Britt, and for what this company means to them. Hold
things together for me until I get back and we can get
this diamond project properly under way and then you'll
see the benefits for both our people.'

'How long will you be away?' The words were out
before she could stop them, and she hated herself for
asking, but then reassured herself that, as this concerned
business, she had to know.

'A month, no more, I promise you that.'

The tension grew and then she said, 'I noticed a lot of new people were here when I arrived. Will you introduce me?'

Sharif visibly relaxed. 'Thank you, Britt,' he said. 'The people you saw are people I trust. People I hope you will learn to trust. They moved in with the approval of your lawyers and with your own financial director alongside them to smooth the path—'

'Of your consortium's takeover of my family's company,' she said ruefully.

'Of our necessary intervention,' Sharif amended. 'I hope I can give you cause to change your mind,' he said when he saw her expression. 'This is going to be good for all of us, Britt—and you of all people must know there's no time to waste. Winter in the Arctic is just around the corner, which will make the preliminary drilling harder, if not impossible, so I need your firm answer now.'

'I'll stay,' she said quietly. 'Of course, I'll stay.'

How ironic it seemed that Sharif was battling to keep her on. He was right, though, she could handle anything the business threw at her, but when it came to her personal life she was useless. She had no self-belief, no courage, no practice in playing up to men, or making them see her as a woman who hurt and cared and loved and worried that she would never be good enough to deserve a family of her own to love, and a partner with whom she shared everything

'And when you come back?' she said.

'You can stay or not, as you please. You can still have an involvement in the company, but you could travel, if that's what you want to do. I have business interests in Kareshi that you are welcome to look over.'

A sop for her agreement, she thought. But a welcome one—if a little daunting for someone whose life had always revolved around Skavanga. 'I'd be like you then, always travelling.'

'And always returning home,' Sharif said with a shrug. 'What can I tell you, Britt? If you want responsibility there is no easy way. You should know that. You have to take everything that comes along.'

'And when Tyr comes home?'

'I'm not sure that your brother has any interest in the business—beyond saving it.'

She flushed at misjudging her brother when she should have known that Tyr would have all their best interests at heart.

'And now I've got a new contract of employment for you—'

'You anticipated my response.' But she went cold. Was she so easy to read? If she was, Sharif must know how hopelessly entangled her heart was with his.

Sharif gave nothing away as he uncapped his pen. 'Your lawyers have given it the once-over,' he explained. 'You can read their letter. I've got it here for you. I'll leave you in private for a few moments.'

She picked it up as Sharif shut the door behind him. Her nerves were all on edge as she scanned the contents of the letter. 'This is the best solution,' jumped out at her. So be it. She drew a steadying breath, knowing there wasn't time for personal feelings. There never had been time. She had consistently fooled herself about that where Sharif was concerned.

Walking to the door, she asked the first person she saw to witness her signature and two minutes later it was done. She issued a silent apology to her ancestors. This was no longer a family firm. She worked for the consortium now like everyone else at Skavanga Mining.

Sharif returned and saw her face. 'You haven't lost anything, Britt. You've only gained from this.'

That remained to be seen, she thought, remembering Sharif leaving her in Kareshi and again at the cabin.

'I left a message for you in Kareshi,' he said as if picking up on these thoughts. 'Didn't you get it? The women? Didn't they come to find you?' he added as she slowly shook her head.

And then she remembered the women trying to speak to her before she left. She'd been in too much of a hurry to spare the time for them. 'They did try to speak to me,' she admitted.

'But you didn't give them chance to explain?' Sharif guessed. 'Like you I never walk away from responsibility, Britt. You should know I would always get a message to you somehow.'

And he was actually paying her a compliment leaving Skavanga Mining in her care. It was a compliment she would gladly park in favour of hearing Sharif tell her that he couldn't envisage life without her—

How far must this self-delusion go before she finally got it into her head that whatever had happened between them in the past was over? Sharif had clearly moved on to the next phase of his life. Why couldn't she?

'Welcome on board, Britt.'

She stared at his outstretched hand, wondering if she dared touch it. She was actually afraid of what she might feel. She sought refuge as always in business. 'Is that it?' she said briskly, turning to go. 'I really should put my sisters out of their misery.'

'They already know what's going on.'

'You told them?'

'Like you, I didn't want them to worry, so I told them what was happening and sent them home.'

'You don't take any chances, do you, Sharif?' She

stared into the dark, unreadable eyes of the man who had briefly been her lover and who was now her boss.

'Never,' he confirmed.

A wave of emotion jolted her as she walked to the door. Sharif's voice stopped her. 'Don't leave like this,' he said.

She turned her face away from him, unwilling to meet his all-seeing stare. The last thing she wanted now was to break down in front of him. Sharif must be given no reason to think she wasn't tough enough to handle the assignment he had tasked her with.

'Britt,' he ground out, his mouth so close to her ear. 'Please. Listen to me—'

She tried to make a joke of it and almost managed to huff a laugh as she wrangled herself free. 'I think I've listened to you enough, don't you?'

'You don't get it, do you?' he said. 'I'm doing this for you—I rushed here for you—to save the company. This isn't just for the consortium. Yes, of course we'll benefit from it, but I wanted to save your company for you. Can't you see that? Why else would I leave my country when there's trouble brewing?'

'I don't know,' she said, shaking her head. 'Everything's happened so fast, I just don't know what to think. I only know I don't understand you.'

'I think you do. I think you understand me very well.'

She would not succumb to Sharif's dark charm. She would not weaken now. The urge to soften against him was overpowering, but if she did that she was lost. She might as well pack up her job and agree to be Sharif's mistress for as long as it amused the Black Sheikh. 'I need to go home and see my sisters.'

'You need to stay here with me,' Sharif argued.

She wanted his arms around her too badly to stay. She

still felt isolated and unsure of herself. She, who took pride in standing alone at the head of her troops, felt as if the ground had been pulled away from her feet today.

'Are you frightened of being alone with me, Britt?' Cupping her chin, Sharif made her look at him and she stared back. He was a warrior of the desert, a man who had fought to restore freedom to his country, and who could have brushed her aside and taken over Skavanga Mining without involving her.

So why hadn't he?

'I asked you a question, Britt? Why won't you answer me?'

Sharif's touch on her face was so seductive it would have been the easiest thing in the world to soften in his arms. 'I'm not frightened of you,' she said, speaking more to herself.

'Good,' he murmured. 'That's the last thing I want.'

But if he could know how frightened she was of the way she felt about him, he would surely count it as a victory. And the longer Sharif held her like this, close yet not too close, the more she longed for his warmth and his strength, and the clearer it became that, for the first time in her life, being Britt Skavanga, lone businesswoman, wasn't enough.

'I've got an idea,' Sharif said quietly as he released her.

'What?' she said cautiously.

'I'd like you the think about working in Kareshi as well as Skavanga— Don't look so shocked, Britt. We live in a small world—'

'It's not that.' Her heart had leapt at the thought, but she still doubted herself, doubted her capabilities, and wondered if Sharif was just saying this to make her feel better.

'It's not that—' Her heart had leapt at the thought, even as doubt crowded in that for some reason Sharif just wanted to make her feel better.

'I have always encouraged people to break down unnecessary barriers so they can broaden their horizons in every way. I'm keen to develop talent wherever I find it, and I'd like you to think about using your interpersonal skills more widely. I know you've always concentrated on Skavanga Mining in the past, and that's good, but while I'm away— Well, please just agree to think about what I've said—'

'I will,' she promised as Sharif moved towards the door.

'One month, Britt. I'll send the jet.'

Anything connected with Sharif was a whirlwind, Britt concluded, her head still reeling as he left the room. He ruled a country— He was a warrior. He was a lover, but no more than that. But Sharif had placed his trust in her, and had put her back in charge of Skavanga mining where she could protect the interests of the people she cared about.

A month, he'd said? She'd better get started.

He had to give her time, he reasoned. He would see Britt again soon—

A month—

He consoled himself with the thought that in between times he could sort out his country and his companies—

To hell with all of it!

Without Britt there was nothing. He'd known that on the flight when every mile he put between them was a mile too far. Without Britt there was no purpose to any of this. What was life for, if not to love and be loved?

CHAPTER FIFTEEN

A MONTH WAS a long time in business, and Britt was surprised at how many of the changes were good. With new blood came new ideas, along with fresh energy for everyone concerned to fire off. The combination of ice and fire seemed to be working well at Skavanga Mining. The Kareshis brought interesting solutions for deep shaft mining, while nothing fazed workers in Skavanga who were accustomed to dealing with extreme conditions on a daily basis. Drilling was already under way, and even Britt's sisters had been reassured by how well everyone was getting on, and how much care, time and money the consortium was putting into preserving the environment. They had always taken their lead from Britt where business was concerned and so when she explained Sharif's plan to them, they were all for her trip to Kareshi—though their teasing she could have done without.

'Oh, come off it,' Eva insisted in Britt's minimalist bedroom at the penthouse, where the sisters were helping Britt pack in readiness for the arrival of Sharif's jet the following day. 'We've seen him now. Don't tell me you're not aching to see your desert sheikh again.'

Aching? If a month was a long time in business, it was infinity when it came to being parted from Sharif.

'He isn't *my* desert sheikh,' she said firmly, ignoring the glances her sisters exchanged. 'And, for your information, this is a business trip.'

'Hence the new underwear,' Leila remarked tongue in cheek.

Business trip?

Business trip, Britt told herself firmly as the limousine that had collected her from the steps of the royal flight, no less, slowed in front of the towering, heavily ornamented golden gates that led into the courtyard in front of Sheikh Sharif's residence in his capital city of Kareshi. She had read during the flight that the Black Sheikh's palace was a world heritage site, and was one of the most authentically restored medieval castles. To Britt it was simply overwhelming. The size of the place was incredible. It was, in fact, more like a fortified city contained within massive walls.

It was one month since she had last seen Sharif. One month in which to prepare herself for pennants flying from ancient battlements, alongside the hustle and bustle of a thriving modern city—but she could never be properly prepared, if only because the contrast was just too stark. And those contrasts existed in the Black Sheikh himself. Respectful of traditional values, Sharif was a forward-thinker, always planning the next improvement for his country.

Excitement wasn't enought to describe her feelings. There was also apprehension. Until she saw Sharif's expression when he saw her again, she couldn't relax. She was prepared for anything, and was already steeling her heart—the same heart that was hammering in her ears as she wondered if Sharif would be wearing his full and splendid regalia—the flowing black robes of the desert king? Or would he be wearing a sombre tailored suit to greet a director of what he had referred to in the press as his most exciting project yet?

Exhaling shakily, she hoped the problems he had referred to in Kareshi had been resolved, because she was bringing him good news from the mine. They were ahead of schedule and there was a lot to talk about. Ready for their first business meeting, she had changed into a modest dress and jacket in a conservative shade of beige on the plane.

Her heart bounced as the steps of the citadel came into view. Somewhere inside that gigantic building Sharif was waiting.

Not inside.

And not wearing black robes, either, she realised as the limousine drew to a halt.

Sharif was dressed for riding in breeches, polo shirt and boots…breeches that moulded his lower body with obscene attention to detail…

'Welcome to my home,' he said, opening the car door for her.

His face was hard to read. He was smiling, but it could easily have been a smile of welcome for a business associate, newly arrived in his country. Forget business—forget everything—her heart was going crazy. 'Thank you,' she said demurely, stepping out.

He was just so damn sexy she couldn't think of anything else to say. Her mind was closed to business, and her wayward body had tunnel vision and could only see one man—and that was the sexy man who knew just how to please her. There was only one swarthy, stubble-shaded face in her field of vision, and one head of unruly, thick black hair, one pair of keenly assessing eyes, one aquiline nose, one proud, smooth brow, one firm, sexy mouth—

Pull yourself together, Britt ordered herself firmly as Sharif indicated that she should mount the steps ahead of him.

There were guards in traditional robes with scimitars hanging at their sides standing sentry either side of the grand entrance doors and she felt overawed as she walked past them into the ancient citadel. Every breath she took seemed amplified and their footsteps sounded like pistol shots in the huge vaulted space. Everything was on a grand scale. It was an imposing marble-tiled hall with giant-sized stained-glass windows. There were sumptuous rugs in all the colours of the rainbow, and the beautifully ornamented furniture seemed to have been scaled for a race of giants. She felt like a mouse that had strayed into the lion's den. The arched ceiling above her head seemed to stretch away to the heavens, and she couldn't imagine who had built it, or how the monstrous stone pillars that supported it had been set in place.

Attendants bowed low as Sharif led her on. Even when he was dressed in riding gear, authority radiated from him. He was a natural leader without any affectation, and—

And she was going there again, Britt realised, reining her feelings in. Each time she saw Sharif she found something more to admire about him, yet his insular demeanor irritated the hell out of her too, even if she accepted that hiding his feelings must be an essential tool of kingship.

'Do you like it?' he said, catching her smile.

She jolted back to full attention, realising that Sharif had been watching her keenly the whole time. 'I think it's magnificent,' she said as a group of men in flowing robes with curving daggers in their belts and prayer beads clicking in their hands bowed low to Sharif.

A hint of cinnamon and some other exotic spices cut the air, a timely reminder of just how far away from home she was, and how they still had quite a few issues to address. She wondered if Sharif would hand her over to some underling soon, leaving their discussions until later. She almost hoped he would to give her chance to get used to this.

'What's amusing you?' he said.

'Just taking it all in,' she said honestly. 'I'm a historic building fanatic,' she admitted, thinking that a safe topic of conversation. 'And this is one of the best I've seen.'

'The main part of the citadel was built in the twelfth century—'

As he went on she realised that Sharif really did mean to be her tour guide. She had no complaints. He was an excellent teacher, as she knew only too well.

He took her into scented gardens while her heart yearned for him to a soundtrack of musical fountains.

'We have always had some of the greatest engineers in the world in Kareshi,' he explained.

And some of the greatest lovers too, she thought. And what else but love could this exquisite courtyard have been designed for? Everything spoke of romance—the intricate mosaic patterns on the floor, the songbirds carolling in the lemon trees, and the tinkling water features. Surely it was the most romantic place on earth?

And as such was completely wasted on her, Britt concluded, as Sharif indicated that they should move on. 'I'll have someone show you your room,' he said.

So that was it. Tour over. Her heart lurched on cue as he raked his wild, unruly hair into some semblance of order. He probably couldn't wait to pass her over to someone else.

'Freshen up and then meet me in ten,' he said.

Oh…

'Unless you're too tired after your journey?'

'I'm not tired.'

'Good. Put something casual on. Jeans—'

She held back on the salute as a group of women clothed in flowing gowns in a multitude of colours appeared out of nowhere. She turned to look over her shoulder as they ushered her away, but Sharif had already gone.

'These are your rooms,' an older woman, who seemed in charge of the rest, explained as Britt gazed around in wonder.

'All of them?' she murmured.

'All of them,' the smiling woman explained. 'My name is Zenub. If you need anything you only have to ask—or call me.' And when Britt looked surprised, she added, 'This is an ancient building, but we have a very modern sheikh. There is an internal telephone system. This room leads into your dressing room and bathroom,' she explained, opening an arched fretted door that might have been made of solid gold, for all Britt knew. The door was studded with gems that seemed real enough, and probably were, Britt concluded, since Sharif had explained that every original feature inside the citadel had been faithfully restored to its former glory.

She was excited to discover that she had her own inner courtyard, complete with fountain and songbirds. The scent from a cluster of orange trees decorated with fat, ripe fruit was incredible while the fretted walls and covered walkways kept everything cool. It was just the type of place to invite exploration—the type of place to linger and to dream. Perhaps it was just as well she didn't have time.

'There are clothes in the wardrobe, should you need them,' Zenub told her as she ushered the other women out. 'And your suitcase is over here,' she added, indicating a dressing room with yet another glorious display of fresh flowers on one of the low-lying, heavily decorated brass tables. 'Please don't hesitate to call me if you need anything else.'

Britt smiled. 'I will—thank you. And thank you for everything you've done to make me so welcome.'

Amazing didn't quite cover this, Britt reflected as the women left her alone in what amounted to the most fabulous apartment. Every item must have been a priceless treasure, and it was only when she walked into the bathroom and smiled that she saw Sharif's hand in the restoration. The bathroom was state of the art too. There were the high-quality towels on heated rails, as well as fabulous products lined up on the shelves. If the harem pavilion in the desert had been a place of pure pleasure, this was sheer indulgence. It was just a shame she didn't have time to indulge. Another time, she mused ruefully, stepping into the shower.

She showered down quickly and dried off. Tying back her hair, she thought, Sharif stipulated casual, so she tugged on her jeans. A simple white tee and sneakers completed the outfit. A slick of lip gloss and a spritz of scent later and she was ready—for anything, she told herself firmly, leaving the room.

Except for the sight of Sharif wearing a tight black top that sculpted his muscular arms to perfection, and snug-fitting jeans secured by a heavy-duty belt, holding heaven in its rightful place.

And why had she never noticed he had a tattoo before? *She'd been otherwise engaged, possibly?*

'Hello,' she managed lamely, while her thoughts ran crazy stupid wild.

'Britt.' He looked her over and seemed pleased. 'You fulfilled the brief.'

'Yes, I did, boss.' She raised her chin and met the dark, appraising stare with a challenging grin.

'Shall we?'

She glanced at the imposing doors, either side of which stood silent guards whose rich, jewel-coloured robes and headdresses reminded her that this was an exciting land full of rich variety and many surprises. But not half as many surprises as the man standing next to her, Britt suspected as they jogged down the steps together. She stopped at the bottom of the steps and did a double take. 'A motorbike?'

Sharif raised a sexy, inky brow. 'I take it you've seen one before?'

'Of course, but—'

'Helmet?'

'Thank you.' She buckled it on.

And yes, there were outriders. And yes, there was an armoured vehicle that might have contained anything from a rocket launcher to a mobile café, but it wouldn't have mattered, because none of the following posse could keep up with Sharif.

Riding a bike was hot without any additional inducements, like jean-clad sheikhs she had to cling to. Sharif was a great rider. She felt safe and yet in terrible danger—in the most thrilling way. By the time he stopped the big machine outside the university he could have had her on the street.

Fortunately, Sharif had more control than she had

and led her through the beautifully groomed grounds, explaining that he wanted to talk to her before he introduced Britt to the students.

'You've got another idea,' she guessed.

'You know me so well,' he said, his dark eyes glinting.

I wish, she thought as Sharif ruffled his hair. 'So, what's it about?'

'We've talked about this before, in a way,' he said, perching on a wall and drawing her down beside him. 'If you agree, I'd like you to start thinking about plans to bring our two countries together by arranging exchange trips between students.'

'Is that why you've brought me here?'

'That's one reason, yes. I want you to see where your diamonds are going.'

She couldn't pretend she wasn't excited. Her world had always revolved around Skavanga, but now Sharif was offering her more—so much more and her heart soared with hope.

'You're the best person for the job,' he said. 'You'll be reporting to me, of course—'

'Oh, of course.' She tried to keep it light.

'Don't mock,' he warned.

He touched her cheek as he said this, and stared deep into her eyes. It was impossible to feel nothing. Impossible, but she tried not to show it.

'Your first task is to work on a way for our people to learn about each other's culture.'

And now the dam finally burst and she laughed. 'Birch twig switches and harem tents? That should go down well with the students—'

'Britt—'

'I know. I'm sorry. I think it's a wonderful idea.' And

she could tell that it meant a lot to Sharif. This wasn't a whim on his part; this was a declaration of sorts—and maybe the only one she would ever get. But they were close. Deep down she knew this. And she wasn't fooling herself this time, because Sharif was sharing some of the things closest to his heart with her, and when he squeezed her hand and smiled into her eyes, she knew how much this meant to Sharif and was honoured to be a part of it.

'You would have to come back to Kareshi, of course,' he said, frowning.

'Of course,' she said thoughtfully.

'Once the changes have been implemented in Skavanga and everything has settled down here, I want you to tour our universities and colleges with me—art galleries, concert halls and museums. I want to share everything with you, Britt.'

'For the sake of the exchange scheme,' she clarified, still lacking something on the confidence front.

'Absolutely,' Sharif agreed. 'We have some fascinating exhibits in the museums. You might even recognise some of them.'

'But you don't expect me to explain those to students, I hope?'

'I don't think they need any explanation, do you?'

She stared into Sharif's laughing eyes, remembering everything in the fabulous pavilion where she had lost her heart. It had never occurred to her that Sharif might have lost his too.

Or was she just kidding herself again?

CHAPTER SIXTEEN

HE STOOD BACK to watch Britt, wanting to remember every single detail as she met and mingled with the students for the first time. He wished then that he had been less preoccupied and more open from the start, so he could have showered her with gifts and told her how he felt about her. But he had been like Britt—all duty, with every hour of every day filled. They had both changed. He had maybe changed most of all when he had discovered that a month away from Britt was like a lifetime. He'd realised then how much she meant to him and had concluded that it must never happen again.

He wondered now if he'd ever seen her truly relaxed before. Britt Skavanga unmasked and laughing was a wonderful creation. She genuinely loved people and would be wasted behind a desk in an office.

They ate together with a crowd of students who swarmed around Britt. He was almost jealous. Their table was the noisiest, but she still got up and went around every table in the refectory, introducing herself and explaining the scheme she was already cooking in her head. It was as if there had never been a misunderstanding between them, he thought as she glanced over to him and smiled as if wanting to reassure him that she was enjoying this. One of the students commented that Britt came from a cold country, but she had a warm heart.

Cheesy, but she'd warmed his heart. How long had he been in love with her? From that first crazy day, maybe? He just hadn't seen it for what it was. But one of the nice things about being a sheikh was that he could pretty much follow his instinct, and his instinct said, don't let this woman go. He had everything in a material sense a man could want, but nothing resonated without Britt. He saw things differently through her eyes. She made every experience richer. He wanted her in his life permanently and that meant not half a world away. He wanted them to do more than plan an exchange scheme or run a company. He was thinking on a much wider scale—a scale that would encompass both their countries. A life together was what he wanted. He knew that now, and that could only benefit the people who depended on them, and for the first time he thought he saw a way to do it.

'Are you ready to go?' he whispered to Britt discreetly.

'Not really,' she admitted with her usual honesty, gazing round at all the people she hadn't had chance to meet yet.

'You can come back,' he promised. 'Remember—I've asked you to run this project, so you're going to be seeing a lot of these people.'

'But—'

As he held her stare she saw with sudden clarity exactly what he was thinking. Her own eyes widened as his gaze dropped to her mouth.

They were never going to make it back to the citadel. He lost the outriders a few streets away from the university and the security van went off radar in a maze

SUSAN STEPHENS 177

of side-turnings in the suburbs. Britt yelled to ask him
what he was he doing when he pulled into a disused
parking lot earmarked for development.

'What do you think?' he yelled back, skidding to
a halt.

The scaffolding was up and a few walls were built,
but that was it. More importantly, no one was working
on the site today. Dismounting, he propped the bike on
its stand and lifted Britt out of the saddle.

'Is this safe?' she demanded when he backed her
against a wall.

'I thought you loved a bit of danger?'

'I do,' she said, already whimpering as he kissed
her neck.

He couldn't wait. Neither could she. Pelvis to pelvis with pressure, waiting was impossible. Fingers flying, they ripped at each other's clothes. Blissful relief
as Britt's legs locked around his waist and her small
strong hands gripped his shoulders. Anything else was
unimportant now. They were together. She was ready
for him—more than. Penetration was fast and complete.
There was a second's pause when they both closed their
eyes to savour the moment, but from then on it was all
sensation. He cupped her buttocks in his hands to prevent them scraping on the gritty wall, as he kissed her.
He groaned and thrust deep, dipping his knees to gain
a better angle. Britt was wild, just as he liked her. He
wanted to shout out—let the world know how he felt
about this woman— How he'd felt without her, which
was empty, lost, useless— And how he felt now—exul-
tant. Nothing could ever express his frustration at how
long it had taken him to realise that if they wanted each
other enough, they would find a way to be together. And
that it had to happen here in a parking lot—

'Sharif?' she said.

She was giving him a worried look he'd seen before; he knew she couldn't hold on. 'Britt...'

He smiled against her mouth, loving the tension that always gripped her before release. And now it was a crazy ride, hands clawing, chests heaving, wild cries, until, finally, blessed release. The best. It wasn't just physical. This was heart and soul. Commitment. He was committed to this woman to the point where even the direction his future took would depend on what she said now.

'Marry me,' he said fiercely. 'Marry me and stay with me in Kareshi.'

'Yes,' she murmured groggily in a state of content-ment, resting heavily against him. '*What?*' she yelped, coming down to earth with a bump.

'Stay with me and be my queen.'

'You *are* joking?'

'No,' he said, brushing her hair back from her face. 'I can assure you I'm not joking.'

'You're a king, proposing marriage in a car lot when you've just had me up against the wall?'

'I'm a man asking a woman to marry me.'

'Aren't you being a little hasty?'

'Crazy things happen in car lots and this has been at the back of my mind for quite some time.'

'Only at the back,' she teased him as he helped her to sort out her clothes. And then she frowned. 'Are you really sure about this?'

'I'm not in the habit of making marriage proposals in car lots, or anywhere else, so, yes, I'm sure. But you're right—' Going down on one knee in the dirt, he asked the question again.

'You *are* sure,' she exclaimed. 'But how on earth will we make this work?'

'You and me can't solve this? Are you serious?'

'But—'

'But nothing,' he said. 'You can travel as I do. You can use the Internet. I don't have any trouble staying in touch.'

'And you run a country,' she mused.

'I'm only asking you to run my life.' He shrugged. 'How hard can that be?'

She gave him a crooked smile. 'I'd say that could be quite a challenge.'

'A challenge I hope you want to take on?' he said, holding her in front of him.

'Yes.'

'I'd be surprised if you'd said anything else,' he admitted, returning the grin as he brushed a kiss against her mouth.

'You arrogant—'

'Sheikhs are supposed to be arrogant,' he said, kissing her again. 'I'm only fulfilling my job description.'

'So I'd be staying here in Kareshi with you?'

'Living with me,' he corrected her. 'And running a very important project—with me, not for me. You'll be working for both our countries, alongside me. We'll be raising a family together, and you'll be my wife. But none of this will take place *here*, exactly. I did have somewhere a little better than a parking lot in mind.'

'What about the harem?'

'I'll tell them to go home.'

'I meant the tent.'

'We'll keep it for weekends. So? What's your answer, Britt?'

'I told you already. Yes. I accept your terms.'

'How about my love?'

'I accept that too—and most willingly,' she teased him, her eyes full of everything he wanted to see. 'I love you,' she shouted, making a flock of heavy-winged birds flap heavily up and away from the scaffolding. 'And I don't care who knows it.'

'And I love you too,' he said, and, drawing her into his arms, he kissed her again. 'I love you more than life itself, Britt Skavanga. Stay with me and help me build Kareshi into somewhere we can both be proud of. And I promise you that from now on there will be no secrets between us.'

But then she frowned again and asked the question he knew was coming.

'How can I ever leave Skavanga?'

'I'm not asking you to leave Skavanga. I'm asking you to be my wife, which will give you more freedom than you've ever dreamed of. You can work alongside me and raise a family. You can be a queen and a director of a company. You can head up charities and run my exchange programmes for me. You can recruit the brightest and the best of the students you've just met. I'm asking you to be my wife, the mother of my children, and my lover. The only restrictions will be those you impose on yourself, or that love imposes on you. You'll find a balance. I know it. And if you want more time—you've got it.'

They linked fingers as they walked back to Sharif's bike. They were close in every way. Her hand felt good in his. She felt good with this man. She felt safe. She felt warm inside. She felt complete.

EPILOGUE

'THERE'S JUST ONE thing missing,' Britt commented wistfully as her sister helped her to dress on her wedding day in her beautiful apartment at the citadel in Kareshi.

'Tyr,' Leila guessed as she lifted the cloud of cobweb-fine silk chiffon that would be attached to the sparkling diadem that would crown Britt's flowing golden hair.

'Have you heard anything? Has Sharif said anything to you about Tyr?' Eva demanded, her sharp tone mellowed somewhat by the hairpins she was holding in her mouth. 'After all, Tyr is a major player in the consortium now.'

'Nothing,' Britt admitted, turning to check her back view in the mirror. 'Sharif shares everything with me, but he won't share that. He says Tyr will return in his own good time, and that Tyr will explain his absence then, and that we must never think the worst of him, because Tyr is doing some wonderful work—'

'Righting wrongs everywhere but here,' Eva remarked.

'You know he's already done that—fighting with Sharif to free Kareshi. And I trust Sharif,' Britt said firmly. 'If he says Tyr will explain himself when he feels the time is right, then he will. And if Sharif has given his word to Tyr that he won't say anything, then he won't—not even to me.'

'So, I suppose we have to be satisfied with that,' Eva commented, standing back to admire her handiwork. 'And I must say those diamonds are fabulous.'

'I'm glad they distracted you,' Britt teased.

'Well, they would, wouldn't they?' Eva conceded. 'And this veil…'

'Eva, I do believe you're looking wistful,' Britt remarked with amusement as her sister reached for Britt's dress. 'Are you picturing yourself on your own wedding day?'

Eva sniffed. 'Don't be so ridiculous. There isn't a man alive I could be interested in.' Eva chose not to notice the look her sisters exchanged. 'Now, let's get this dress on you,' she said. 'The way Sharif runs you ragged with all those projects he's got you involved in, it will probably drop straight off you again.'

As Leila sighed even Eva was forced to give a pleased and surprised hum. 'Well… Who knew you could look so girlie?' she said with approval, standing back.

'Only a sister,' Britt muttered, throwing Eva a teasing fierce look while Leila tut-tutted at their exchange.

'Eva!' Leila complained where her two sisters settled down for a verbal sparring match. 'You can't get into a fight with Britt on her wedding day.'

'More's the pity,' Eva muttered, advancing with the veil.

'The dress fits like a dream,' Leila reassured Britt.

'Stand still, will you?' Eva ordered Britt. 'How am I supposed to fix this tiara to your head?'

'With a hammer and nails, in your present mood?' Britt suggested, exchanging a grin with Leila.

But Eva was right in one thing—the past six months

had been hectic. She had overseen so many exciting new schemes, as well as flying back to Skavanga to manage the ongoing work there. And as if that wasn't enough, she had insisted on having a hand in the organisation of her wedding at the citadel. Some people never knew when to relax the reins, Sharif had told her, with the type of smile that could distract her for quite a while. She wouldn't have it any other way, Britt reflected. Life had never been so rich, and when the baby came...

Tracing the outline of her stomach beneath the fairytale gown, she knew she would keep on working until Sharif tied her to the bed. Actually—

'Man alert,' Leila warned before Britt had chance to progress this delicious thought.

'Don't worry, I won't let him in,' Leila assured her.

'Stand back, I'll handle this,' Eva instructed her younger sister. Marching to the door, her red hair flying, Eva swung it open. 'Yes?'

There was silence for a moment and Britt turned to see who could possibly silence her combative middle sister.

'Ladies, please excuse me, but the bridegroom has asked me to deliver this gift to his beautiful bride.'

The voice was rich, dark chocolate, and even Britt could see that the man himself was just as tempting. Eva was still staring at him transfixed as Leila stepped forward to take the ruby red velvet box he was holding out.

'Thank you very much,' Britt said politely, taking another look at the man and then at Eva. Which one would blink first? she wondered.

'It is my pleasure,' he said, switching his attention back to Britt. 'Count Roman Quisvada at your service...'

He bowed? He bowed. 'And this is my sister, Leila,'

she said, remembering her manners. 'And Eva…' Who, of course, had to tip her stubborn little chin and glance meaningfully from the count to the door.

'I can see you're very busy,' the handsome Italian said, taking the hint, his dark eyes flashing with amusement. 'I hope to spend more time with you later.'

'Was he looking at me when he said that?' Eva demanded huffily, her cheeks an attractive shade of pink, Britt thought, as Eva closed the door behind the count with a flourish.

'There's no need to sound so peeved,' Leila pointed out. 'He's hot. And he's polite.'

'I do like a man who's polite in the bedroom,' Britt commented tongue in cheek.

'Wow, wow, wow,' Leila whispered as Britt opened the lid of the velvet box. 'And there's a note,' she added as the three Skavanga sisters stared awestruck at the blue-white diamond heart hanging from a finely worked platinum chain; the diamond flashing fire in all the colours of the rainbow.

Britt read the note while her sisters read over her shoulder: *I hope you enjoy wearing the first polished diamond to come from the Skavanga mine. It's as flawless as you are. Sharif.*

'Cheese-ee,' Eva commented. 'And he doesn't know you very well.'

Britt shook her head as the three sisters laughed.

When she walked down the red-carpeted steps towards him, the congregation in the grand ceremonial hall faded away, and there was only Britt— Beautiful Britt. His bride. But she was so much more than that and they were so much more together than they were apart.

'You look beautiful,' he murmured as her flame-haired sister and the young one, Leila, peeled away.

Now there were just the two of them he didn't dare
to look at her or he'd carry her away and to hell with
everyone. It took all he'd got to repeat the vows pa-
tiently and clearly when all the time his arms ached to
hold her. Britt's darkening eyes said she felt the same,
and as she held his gaze to tease him she knew how
that would test him.

His control was definitely being severely tested, but
that was one of the things he loved about Britt. She challenged him on every front and always had.

And long may it continue, he thought, teasing her
back by staring fixedly ahead.

Sharif in heavy black silk robes perfumed with Sandalwood and edged with gold was a heady sight.

And he was her husband...

Her husband, Britt reflected, feeling a volcanic excitement rising inside her. Could she contain her lust?
Sharif was refusing to look at her and it was only when
they were declared man and wife that he finally turned.

Now she knew why he'd refused to look at her. The
fire in his eyes was enough to melt her bones. How
was she going to stand this? How was she going to sit
through the wedding breakfast?

The food was delicious, but even that wasn't enough
of a distraction. The setting was unparalleled, but nothing could take her mind off the main event. Candles
flickered in golden sconces, casting a mellow glow
over the jewel-coloured hangings, making golden plates
and goblets flash as if they were on fire, while crystal glasses twinkled like fireflies dancing through the
night. It was a voluptuous feast, prepared by world-re-
nowned chefs, but she wondered if it would ever end,
and was surprised when Sharif stood up.

'Ladies and gentlemen,' he began in the deep husky

voice Sharif could use to seduce to command. 'The evening is young, and I urge you to enjoy everything to the full. Thank you all for coming to help us celebrate this happiest of days, but now I must beg you to excuse us—'

She still didn't quite understand until Sharif whistled up his horse and held out his hand to her. His black stallion galloped into the hall. As *coup de théâtre* went, she had to admit this one was unparalleled. As their guests gasped the stallion skidded to a halt within inches of its master, and the next thing she knew Sharif was lifting her onto the saddle and holding her safely in front of him.

She gasped as the stallion reared, his silken mane flowing like liquid black diamonds, as his flashing ebony hooves clawed imperiously at the air.

The instant he touched down again, Sharif gave a command in the harsh tongue of Kareshi, and the horse took them galloping out of the hall into a starlit night, and a future that was sure to fulfil all their desires.

* * * * *

&

A sneaky peek at next month...

MODERN™

INTERNATIONAL AFFAIRS, SEDUCTION & PASSION GUARANTEED

My wish list for next month's titles...

In stores from 21st June 2013:

☐ His Most Exquisite Conquest – Emma Darcy
☐ His Brand of Passion – Kate Hewitt
☐ The Couple who Fooled the World – Maisey Yates
☐ Proof of Their Sin – Dani Collins
☐ In Petrakis's Power – Maggie Cox

In stores from 5th July 2013:

☐ One Night Heir – Lucy Monroe
☐ The Return of Her Past – Lindsay Armstrong
☐ Gilded Secrets – Maureen Child
☐ Once is Never Enough – Mira Lyn Kelly

Available at WHSmith, Tesco, Asda, Eason, Amazon and Apple

Just can't wait?

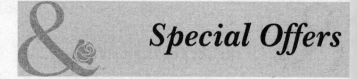

Special Offers

Every month we put together collections and longer reads written by your favourite authors.

Here are some of next month's highlights— and don't miss our fabulous discount online!

On sale 21st June   On sale 5th July   On sale 5th July

Save 20%
on all Special Releases

Find out more at
www.millsandboon.co.uk/specialreleases

Visit us Online

0713/ST/MB422

Join the Mills & Boon Book Club

Want to read more **Modern**™ books?
We're offering you **2 more** absolutely **FREE!**

We'll also treat you to these fabulous extras:

- 🌹 **Exclusive offers and much more!**

- 🌹 **FREE home delivery**

- 🌹 **FREE books and gifts with our special rewards scheme**

Get your free books now!

visit www.millsandboon.co.uk/bookclub
or call Customer Relations on 020 8288 2888

The World of Mills & Boon®

There's a Mills & Boon® series that's perfect for you. We publish ten series and, with new titles every month, you never have to wait long for your favourite to come along.

Scorching hot, sexy reads
4 new stories every month

By Request

Relive the romance with the best of the best
9 new stories every month

Cherish™

Romance to melt the heart every time
12 new stories every month

Desire™

Passionate and dramatic love stories
8 new stories every month